Everly stood in the middle of the living room.

The unmistakable glint of a metal blade was at her neck. The perpetrator was hidden behind her, face obscured. Wyatt's heart beat in triple time. His palms grew damp and a bead of sweat trickled down his back.

He inhaled and exhaled, slowing his racing heart. There were only two things Wyatt needed to do: save Everly's life and catch the serial killer. Good thing he'd brought a gun to a knife fight.

"Drop that blade or I'll shoot," he said, remaining hidden in the shadows.

The knife flashed, gouging Everly's skin. Like a seam had opened, a bead of red blood gathered on her cheek. She shrieked. A shadow took form and rushed from the room. The back door shut with a crack.

Wyatt sprinted through the living room and pushed against the door. It didn't budge. He fumbled with the doorknob and leaned his shoulder into the door, knowing it was a smart move on the intruder's part. Barricade the door. Wyatt was trapped—a prisoner in his own home.

* * *

Dear Reader,

I am beyond thrilled to continue the Rocky Mountain Justice series. Yet, there is one person who I need to thank above all others—and that is you, Dear Reader! As excited as I am that I get to continue to write the RMJ series, the exhilaration pales in comparison to the fact that the previous books were enjoyed by readers everywhere. I'm sure you've heard before that writing is a solitary endeavor. While that is somewhat true, authors don't publish books to stay hidden. In fact, we write because we are driven to share our stories.

Thank you, Dear Reader, for giving all of the Rocky Mountain Justice books a place in the world.

Under the Agent's Protection, along with the subsequent four books in the miniseries, began with an editor's single suggestion: *You know what we'd love to see? A serial killer.*

That seed took root in my imagination. It was watered with a good bit of research and interviews about the formation of serial killers and what drives those who study and pursue them. In writing this book, I was forced to ask a very personal question: What frightens me the most? Rocky Mountain Justice expanded from Colorado and took up residence in the small town of Pleasant Pines, Wyoming. To all of that I added four separate love stories, and this newest miniseries flourished! As always, it is my honor to create smart and sexy books for you, Dear Reader. I hope you enjoy reading *Under the Agent's Protection* as much as I enjoyed writing it!

Regards,

Jennifer D. Bokal

UNDER THE AGENT'S PROTECTION

Jennifer D. Bokal

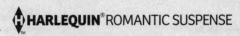

HARLEQUIN® ROMANTIC SUSPENSE

Recycling programs
for this product may
not exist in your area.

ISBN-13: 978-1-335-66219-4

Under the Agent's Protection

Copyright © 2019 by Jennifer D. Bokal

Printed in U.S.A.

Jennifer D. Bokal is the author of the bestselling ancient-world historical romance *The Gladiator's Mistress* and the second book in the Champions of Rome series, *The Gladiator's Temptation*. Happily married to her own alpha male for twenty years, she enjoys writing stories that explore the wonders of love in many genres. Jen and her husband live in upstate New York with their three beautiful daughters, two aloof cats and two very spoiled dogs.

Books by Jennifer D. Bokal

Harlequin Romantic Suspense

Wyoming Nights
Under the Agent's Protection

Rocky Mountain Justice
Her Rocky Mountain Hero
Her Rocky Mountain Defender
Rocky Mountain Valor

Visit the Author Profile page at Harlequin.com for more titles.

To John. You are always the one.

Prologue

Wyatt Thornton cocked back his arm as far as he could, then released his grip. The stick somersaulted through the air. Kicking up the remnants of last winter's snow, his dog, Gus, barked happily and gave chase. The land, these miles of foothills in the Rocky Mountains, belonged to Wyatt. It was more than a home, it was a refuge—his place of escape, where the world hardly knew he existed.

A place he could truly be alone.

Gus returned and dropped the slobbery branch at Wyatt's feet. After ruffling the Lab's ears, Wyatt once again picked up the stick. This time, he threw it harder, sending it sailing through the clear blue sky. With another excited bark, Gus raced after it, disappearing into the woods.

Turning his face to the sun, Wyatt closed his eyes and inhaled deeply. He'd never gotten used to the sweet, fresh Wyoming air—not when compared to the miasma of exhaust fumes, cigarettes and sunscreen he had lived with for more than a decade in Las Vegas. The scents of the Strip, everyone used to joke. After exhaling fully, Wyatt again inhaled. A primal wail shot through the silent morning and his breath caught in his chest.

"Gus?"

Heart pounding and legs pumping, Wyatt rushed between the shadows cast by the towering trees.

"Gus," he called. "Where are you, boy?"

He heard a yelp in the distance and his chest contracted. All the dangers that might have befallen his faithful companion came to him in one horrifying rush. A newly awake and hungry bear. An unseen ditch and the dog's broken paw. Poor footing on a slope that ended with Gus maimed at the bottom of a ravine.

He stopped and listened. The silence was total, not even interrupted by the whisper of a breeze.

"Gus? Where are you?"

His call was answered with a bark. The noise ricocheted off the hills, coming from everywhere and nowhere at once. Wyatt stopped and focused.

The first bark was followed by another, this one louder and definitely from his right. Wyatt's pulse spiked, and he followed the sound up a hill. The soft ground crumbled underfoot, and he scrambled on hands and knees to the top of the rise. One hundred yards in the distance stood the old schoolhouse, the farthest point on his land.

Made up of a single room, the century-old stone foundation was still intact. There was a hole in the ceiling where part of the roof had collapsed in the corner. Gus stood on the threshold, whole and healthy. He barked, and his tail was a wagging blur.

Wyatt wiped his hands on the seat of his pants, while his racing heartbeat slowed. "There you are," he said between breaths as he half jogged to the schoolhouse. "Come here."

Gus barked again. With a whine, the dog looked over his shoulder.

"What is it, boy?" Wyatt asked.

Gus darted into the dilapidated building. Wyatt approached and stopped short, recognizing the smell of decay. It was like the rot of a slaughterhouse, but stronger.

Swallowing down his deepest sense of revulsion, he stepped slowly into the structure.

Gus stood near a far corner and pawed at the floor. Behind the dog was the unmistakable form of a corpse.

"Easy, boy," Wyatt said to his dog. With a slap to his thigh, he added, "Come here."

With one last look at the lump on the floor, Gus moved to his master's side.

No matter how long he'd been out of the game, the skills Wyatt had developed over years of training rose to the surface. He began to catalogue all the details—some obvious, others more subtle.

The deceased was male and Caucasian. His age appeared to be between 25 and 40—quite a range, but a wild animal had gotten to his face and throat, making a more exact guess impossible. Wyatt looked around for blood splatter on the walls or floor.

There was nothing.

Wyatt moved in for a closer look, kneeling next to the body.

Dressed in a flannel shirt, down-filled coat and lined denim jeans, John Doe wore the same outfit as three quarters of the state of Wyoming. What made him interesting were the accessories—his hiking boots were high-quality and retailed for over 700 dollars per pair. Wyatt knew that fact as he had a pair himself. The treads were worn, and the tops were scarred with scuff marks. John Doe also wore a top-of-the-line smartwatch. The screen was blank.

But there was no visible sign of trauma. No blackened bullet hole to the chest. No knife wound to the side, crusted over with blood. It was almost as if this man had wandered into the abandoned schoolhouse and died.

No, Wyatt thought, correcting his thinking, there was no *almost* about it.

Cardiac arrest? Perhaps.

Wyatt began to question the scenario before him. Perhaps John Doe—a wealthy tourist, no doubt—had lost his way while hiking in the mountainous terrain. Maybe he'd sought shelter from the frigid temperatures in the old schoolhouse. But in the mountains, it wouldn't have been enough.

The lack of snow was deceptive. The last few nights the temperature had dropped into the low twenties, maybe even high teens. Either way, it was cold enough for someone to die from exposure. It happened all the time, so much so that it was hardly news anymore.

Then again, there were other things that Wyatt would've expected to see and didn't. He touched the flagstone floor. It was smooth, cold and inexplicably spotless. Wyatt inspected the corpse's hands. The fingernails were clean and smooth. It meant that John Doe had hardly struggled in the wild to survive.

No footprints.

No injuries.

No clues.

He pulled a wallet from the man's back pocket and checked for I D. There was an Illinois driver's license in the name of Axl Baker. Conflicting feelings of trepidation and adrenaline dropped into Wyatt's gut. It was the same feeling he had at the beginning of every new case. And even though the scene felt familiar, this time it was different. This time, Wyatt would have nothing more to do with the dead guy on the floor.

Because Wyatt Thornton had left the FBI for a good reason. And nothing, not even an unexplained death, could force him back to work.

Chapter 1

The radio in Sheriff Carl Haak's truck crackled a moment before the 911 dispatcher's voice came through. "You there, Sheriff?" she asked.

Carl looked at the clock on the dashboard. It wasn't even 7:00 in the morning yet. He lifted the radio's handset and pressed the talk button. He continued driving as he said, "Go ahead, Rose."

"A call came in. A body's been found in the old schoolhouse."

Carl's shoulders pinched together with tension and he eased the truck to the side of the road. He only had a couple of weeks left until retirement and looking into another death was not how he wanted to spend his time. Pushing his cowboy hat, emblazoned with a sheriff's tin star on the band, back on his head, he asked, "A body? Whose?"

"A man by the name of Axl Baker. All the way from Chicago, Illinois."

"What happened?"

"Don't know, but the guy who found him didn't think that it was foul play, if that's what worries you."

"What guy?"

"The one who bought the Hampton place a few years back," said Rose. "Wyatt Thornton."

The Hampton family hadn't owned the sprawling piece of land for decades and still Carl knew exactly what property Rose meant. In fact, he passed it every day as he drove to work. "Not foul play? How does Mr. Thornton know?"

"He said there was no sign of injury and that Axl Baker probably died of exposure."

Rose's voice was wistful, and Carl knew why. Ever since Wyatt Thornton had moved to the area several years ago, he'd mostly kept to himself. That didn't mean that his rare appearances in town didn't cause a commotion—amongst the local women, at least. She continued, "He was so sweet on the phone. As nice as he is handsome. He almost reminds me of a movie star."

"What would your husband think of you being sweet on Mr. Thornton?"

"Wyatt," she corrected. "He told me to call him Wyatt, and by the way, Carl, it doesn't do any harm to look. You know, I'm not dead yet."

Carl ignored Rose's comment. Pressing down on

the radio's handset, he asked, "How'd he know it was a natural death? Is he a doctor or something?"

The radio was filled with static, as if Rose was no longer on the other end of the call. The silence stretched. In reality, Carl knew next to nothing about Wyatt Thornton. When the other man first arrived in Pleasant Pines, Sheriff Haak thought about digging into his past.

Yet, Thornton didn't drink, fight, drive too fast or even listen to his music too loud. In short, he was a model citizen. The job of sheriff was a busy one, more important cases arose and Carl never did get around to investigating Thornton.

Now, he wondered if that decision, made long ago, had been for the best.

Finally, Rose answered. "Honestly," she said, "I don't know. He just seemed positive, that's all." Another pause. "He's waiting at the old schoolhouse."

Pressing the talk button, Carl said, "Find out what you can about the victim."

"Sure thing, Carl."

Turning on his lights and siren, Carl swung the truck around on the empty road and dropped his foot on the accelerator. Fifteen minutes later, he was at the turnoff for the old schoolhouse. It was just a wide spot in a dilapidated barbwire fence with low scrub on what used to be a well-worn path.

The ground was covered with frost, and his truck's undercarriage passed well above any dead bushes or brambles. In the distance stood the one-room building. As he got closer, he saw Thornton and his dog standing by the door.

"Just two weeks," he mumbled to himself. Then Carl would be moving to South Carolina, where it was warm all the time and there was a beach two blocks from his tiny condominium. He put the truck in Park and killed the engine. The lights went dim and the siren fell silent.

Stepping into the cold, he shrugged on his jacket. The smell of death permeated the air.

"Morning, Mr. Thornton," he said.

Thornton stepped forward, offering his hand. "Call me Wyatt."

They shook, then the sheriff turned to business. "Well, Wyatt, can you tell me what happened?"

Wyatt gave a succinct rundown of his typical morning walk that today, ended with the dog finding the body. He concluded with, "There's no signs of trauma, so I don't think it's murder."

Carl hefted up his jeans by the belt loops. "How can you know that?"

"Experience," said the other man.

Carl waited for a moment for more information. None was offered. "You a doctor, or something?" he asked, repeating his original assumption.

Wyatt shook his head. "No, I'm not a doctor."

"A movie star?"

Thornton gave a quiet chuckle. "Not a movie star, either." After a beat, he added, "I used to work for the Behavioral Sciences Unit of the FBI."

"You got any identification that says so?" Carl asked.

"What? That says I used to work for the Bureau? I still have my old creds. You can stop by and see them if you want."

"I might do just that. Then again," said Carl, "I'm retiring soon. Two weeks then I'm off to South Carolina."

He waited for Wyatt to say something or offer the expected congratulations. Thornton said nothing. Carl cleared his throat. "One thing I know is that Rose will be excited to hear that we have a real-life G-man in Pleasant Pines."

"If you don't mind," said Wyatt with a lifted palm, "I'd like to keep my former career in the past."

With a nod, Carl said, "I respect a man of discretion."

Wyatt gestured with his chin to the schoolhouse. "Sheriff, you should probably get a look at the scene."

Wyatt walked through the front door and stopped. Carl followed. His gaze was drawn to the corpse at the far side of the room. A dead eye, gone milky white, stared straight at Carl.

Shaking off the skittering sensation that crawled up his spine, he got to work examining the body and the scene. Sure, he'd seen a few deaths in his time on the job—but something about this one just felt *wrong*.

"If you don't mind," said Wyatt. "I want to point out one thing."

"What is it?" asked Carl.

"The floor's clean," Wyatt said.

A beam of sunlight shone from a hole in the roof, illuminating the interior of the structure. Where Carl would've normally seen dirt and debris, there was nothing. "Odd," he agreed. "I would expect at least some dirt collected in a place like this."

"Me, as well," said Wyatt.

"How'd you get a name for the corpse?" Carl asked.

"I found his wallet in his pants pocket. He has a license from Illinois. I left it next to the body."

Carl walked inside and found the wallet. Flipping it open, he found the driver's license, complete with a picture. He looked back at the body. Even with the post-mortem injuries, they were undoubtedly the same man. Legally speaking, it was all he needed to make a positive identification on a John Doe. Standing, Carl dusted his hands on the seat of his pants. "Looks like this is Axl Baker."

"I don't want to disturb anything more than I already have. So, unless you need me," Wyatt said while stepping toward the door, "I'll be on my way."

"I have to get an official statement," said Carl. He followed outside. "Stop by my office tomorrow morning at eleven o'clock."

"I'll see you then," said Wyatt. He called his dog and set off.

Carl watched until they disappeared below the crest of the hill. Returning to his truck, he picked up the radio. "Rose, you there?"

"I am, Sheriff. What d'you need?"

"Call Doc Lambert. I need him to come out and pick up the body."

"Sure thing," she said. "Anything else?"

"Did you get a next of kin for Axl Baker?"

"I did. It's his sister, one Everly Baker, also of Chicago."

Carl scribbled Everly's number on a scrap of paper before signing off. He pulled his cell phone out of his pocket. Even here, there was a strong signal. He entered the number and held his breath. A woman answered the call.

"Yes?"

"Everly Baker?"

"Yes." Her voice rose an octave. "Who is this?"

"Ms. Baker." Carl paused. His temples began to throb, and he held his breath. Calls like this were the worst part of his job. With an exhale, he said, "This is Sheriff Haak in Pleasant Pines, Wyoming. I'm sorry to be bothering you, but I have some awful news…"

The following day

To Everly Baker, it looked as if Pleasant Pines had been carved out of the forest. Pine trees ringed the perimeter, and the center of town was taken up by a village green, complete with a gazebo. Wrought iron lampposts stood on each corner.

There had been a sign, welcoming all visitors and proclaiming that the population was a mere 3,200 people.

The streets were lined with businesses—a grocery store, a diner, a dentist's office and the regional newspaper. People moved about, busy with their own lives. It looked as though not much had changed in the sleepy town for years. A spring snow had started, the flakes swirling across the road. Everly would've found the scene charming, if not for the circumstances.

After receiving the sheriff's call about her brother, she'd caught a flight from Chicago to Cheyenne. From there, Everly rented a car for the last leg of her journey. After almost twenty-four hours of travel, she decided that Pleasant Pines was more than secluded—it was actually cut off from the rest of the world.

Driving down Main Street, Everly shuddered. She still couldn't believe that this nightmare was real. Axl, dead? How could that be? The very idea that her brother was gone forever—and she was all alone in the world—was too overwhelming to handle.

Easing her car into a parking place, Everly turned off the engine. Her throat tightened as a fresh wave of anguish rose from her gut. She drew in a deep breath and waited for the grief to pass.

Using the rearview mirror, she checked her appearance quickly. Her green eyes—puffy. Cheeks—blotchy. Lips—colorless. For the day, she'd swept her hair into a ponytail and a tendril of auburn hair had come loose. Everly was far from put-together. But then again, what did she expect? She'd gotten the call as she was getting ready for work, and still wore the same clothes she'd changed into—black leggings, shearling-lined boots and a long cream-colored sweater.

It was 11:10 a.m. She'd reached her destination with twenty minutes to spare until her meeting with the sheriff.

She hoped that it gave her enough time for a quick detour—even if it wasn't as much as she wanted. Years of experience in public relations had taught Everly to never attend an important meeting without getting all the facts. And as far as Everly was concerned, there was nothing more important than finding out what really happened to her brother.

After draping her purse across her forearm, she hustled through the biting wind to the hospital, situated two blocks from the town square. She followed signs to the morgue, which was located in the basement. The slap of footfalls on the tiled floor kept time with her racing heart as she descended the stairs.

Cold sweat covered her brow as she walked down the white-tiled hallway. A blue plastic sign hung, suspended by chains from the ceiling. Morgue. A metal door was the only thing that separated Everly from the truth. With a deep breath, she pushed open the door and stepped in.

A row of metal tables bisected the large room. There was a figure on the center table, shrouded with a blue sheet.

Sure, the sheriff had told Everly that her brother's body had been found. And yeah, the body had Axl's ID. Yet, she couldn't help but wonder—what if it wasn't Axl under the sheet? What if this had all been a mistake? Because there was one thing Everly knew for sure—her brother didn't die of exposure as the sheriff suggested was the most likely possibility.

She reached out with a shaking hand. Her fingertips inched closer to the sheet, brushing the fabric.

"May I help you?" A man with sparse hair, glasses and a goatee stood next to the sink at the far side of the room.

Everly gasped and pulled her hand away, startled. She took in a deep breath and let it out slowly as her racing heart slowed.

"I hope so," she said. "I'm Everly Baker, Axl Baker's sister. I spoke to Sheriff Haak yesterday and he informed me that I needed to identify my brother's body." Her voice faltered slightly on the last words, and she took another breath to steady her emotions.

"I'm Doc Lambert, ma'am, and very sorry for your loss." The man picked up a clipboard and lifted a sheet of paper. He looked up over the rim of his glasses. "I didn't expect you until after noon, but once the sheriff arrives, we can make the ID."

"Are you the medical examiner?"

"Medical examiner. Pediatrician. General practitioner. Sometimes surgeon."

"If you don't mind, I'd like to see my brother now," she said.

"It's not the way Sheriff Haak likes things done," said Dr. Lambert. "Besides, if the sheriff told you to meet him here, I'm sure he'll be along directly."

"He's not coming right now," said Everly, knowing that the doctor misunderstood her early arrival. Moreover, being direct was the only way to deal with the situation. "But I'm here now."

Still looking over the rims of his glasses, he repeated, "Like I said, Miss Baker, it's not how we do things in Pleasant Pines."

"I have to be honest with you. I think there's been a mistake."

"Mistake? How?"

"I don't think this is my brother." She gestured to the figure on the table.

"We found an ID with the body. He'd checked into the local hotel and used a credit card in his name."

"But aren't I here to see the…corpse and make a positive identification? To me, that means there's a question."

"There is some postmortem gouging to the face." Doc Lambert paused. "Maybe I should call the sheriff."

"Is there a rule in Wyoming that says a law-enforcement officer needs to be present to see a body?"

"Well, no. It's just that Sheriff Haak is particular about his cases."

"No offense," said Everly, knowing full well that she was being persistent—possibly too persistent, "but I'm pretty particular about knowing whether my brother is dead or not."

With a sigh, Doc Lambert set aside his clipboard. "Since it's not against the law, I suppose there's no harm." He moved to the table and pulled the sheet from the body, exposing the head, neck and shoulders.

Everly's chest constricted. A great wave of grief washed over her, threatening to drown her. She reached out to touch her brother's hair then pulled her hand away as the urge to scream flooded through her, pushing its way up into her throat. Yet, she stood without breathing and stared at his lifeless body.

"It's him," she whispered. "That's my brother." It was like a physical blow, acknowledging that he was, indeed, gone for good. "What happened?"

"I won't know until I conduct the autopsy and get some test results back, but it looks as though your brother got caught out in the forest at night and died of exposure. It is fairly common in these parts. Heartbreaking, but natural."

The loss of her brother—her rock for so many years—was unspeakably painful. She didn't know why or how, but Everly was certain of one thing: Doc Lambert was wrong. Her brother's death wasn't natural.

And she was going to find out what really happened to him.

Doc Lambert had given Everly directions to the county office building, only a few short blocks away. It was located on the town square in a three-story granite building, complete with pillars and arched windows. She found the sheriff's office on the second floor and pulled the door open.

A man with dark hair and eyes stood just inside,

his hand outstretched, as if he'd been about to reach for the knob. His abrupt appearance aggravated her already frayed nerves. Her heart slammed into her chest as she jumped back. Her purse wobbled on her arm, and her phone and keys fell onto the floor in the corridor. She bent to get them, and the rest of the contents—lipstick, sunglasses, wallet, receipts, chewing gum—spilled out.

"Damn." She dropped to her knees.

The man let the door to the sheriff's office close and kneeled down next to her. "Let me help you with that," he said.

She reached for her phone in the same instant as the sexy stranger. His fingers grazed the back of her hand. A shiver of awareness traveled up her arm, leaving gooseflesh in its wake.

She jerked her phone away. "Thanks," she grumbled. "I can manage."

"No, really."

He handed her a tube of lipstick. "It was my fault."

With a shake of her head, she said, "It's nobody's fault." She sighed. "I just don't need any help. Okay?"

The man lifted his hands in surrender. "Okay." And yet, he didn't leave.

As Everly scooped the rest of her belongings into her bag, she examined him from beneath her lashes. He was tall, well over six feet. His shoulders were broad and, beneath the fabric of his shirt, she could see the outline of his muscular biceps. Without question, he was more than just attractive—he was achingly handsome. His eyes were a rich and deep brown. He wore a plaid flannel shirt with tones that matched his eyes. He also had on a burnt orange vest—his look was rugged and yet, casually trendy.

Despite everything, Everly's heart gave a flutter.

His outfit was hardly anyone's idea of a uniform. But in an out-of-the-way place like Pleasant Pines, Wyoming, who knew?

"Are you Sheriff Haak?" Her voice trembled as an electric charge danced across her skin.

"Sorry, no." The man smiled and hitched his chin toward the office behind him. "He's in there."

Everly's face flamed red and hot. She had no reason to be embarrassed for the mistake, and yet she was. Immediately, she knew why. She'd been hoping all along that the tall, dark and gorgeous stranger might be the local law in these parts.

What a cliché.

The stranger stood and held out his palm to Everly. She ignored the offered hand and stood as well, taking time to zip her purse closed. Gaze still on the floor, Everly's eyes burned with tears that threatened to fall. How could she feel anything beyond miserable? When she looked up, the man was walking down the hallway.

Exhaling heavily, Everly entered the sheriff's office. Two desks, both empty, sat next to windows that overlooked the town square and gazebo. At the back of the room was an inner office with the sheriff's name stenciled onto the glass panel of the door with black paint.

Sitting behind his desk, Sheriff Haak wore a dark

brown uniform and a khaki-colored tie. A six-sided tin star and gun completed his outfit. In his sixties, balding and with a definite paunch, he looked much more like a grandfather than the Adonis she had just run into. Everly decided it was all for the best that she not let anything distract her from her goal—finding out what really happened to Axl.

"Ms. Baker, I presume," said the sheriff as he rose from his seat. He waved her into his office. "I'm sorry to meet under such terrible circumstances."

Everly approached and tried to speak, but sadness strangled her words and she just nodded.

"Sit, please," said Sheriff Haak as he gestured to a chair opposite his desk. As she sat, he reached for an opened folder. "An autopsy is required in Wyoming to determine cause of death. First, you'll need to see the body and give an identification. I warn you, it may be difficult—"

"I know," said Everly, interrupting what she imagined was a well-worn speech. "I've already been to the morgue."

"Beg your pardon?"

"I met with Doc Lambert and identified the body." She sighed. "It's my brother's."

"That's not how we do things around here," said the sheriff.

"I heard," said Everly, "I'm not interested in procedures. Only in finding out what happened to Axl."

"Doc Lambert is as good a medical man as you'll find anywhere, and will conduct a full examination. After that, you can take your brother's body back to

Illinois. I'd have to say that the ME's findings will
be like mine. Sadly, we have several cases like this
each year—tourists who don't understand the danger
of the mountains. The way I see it, your brother died
of exposure and his death was accidental."

"You're wrong," she said.

The sheriff spluttered. "I'm what?"

She had gone through the scenario several times
in her mind, but now that she had the chance to
plead her case the reasoning seemed thin. No, she
reminded herself. It wasn't her case. She was here for
Axl. And Everly would be damned if she was going
to let a small-town sheriff talk her out of what she
knew to be true.

"My brother was an experienced outdoorsman. He
worked as a wildlife photographer," she continued.
"He was here for his job—and more than that, he'd
never wander off alone. He was murdered." There,
she'd said it.

"Hold on a second." The sheriff poked the desk
with his finger. "With all due respect—this isn't
some big city, where folks get shot on every corner.
Pleasant Pines is a nice, quiet town with nice people,
and I've kept them all safe for decades." The sheriff
leaned forward, his tone softening. "I'm sure this is
all very hard for you to accept."

"My brother had been a wildlife photographer for
more than twelve years. Even if he did end up lost
on a cold night, he'd know what to do." Everly knew
she had to convince the man. "My brother has pho-
tographed Alaska's Denali National Park in winter.

He's also done photo shoots of Death Valley at noon in July." She pressed on. "What about his camera? Did you look at the pictures he'd taken so far? There might be some kind of photographic evidence."

The sheriff leaned forward in his chair. "There wasn't a camera found with the body," he said pointedly.

Everly went numb. She'd given Axl a top-of-the-line camera for his thirtieth birthday two years ago. It cost as much as her last month's rent and he kept it with him always. "Are you sure?"

The sheriff slid a piece of paper across the desk. "This is the list of all his belongings from the scene. I catalogued everything myself. There's no camera."

Her pulse began to hammer, and her breath froze in her chest. She scanned the list, not seeing anything. "This doesn't make any sense. If my brother wasn't taking pictures, why was he outside in the middle of the night?"

"Even a seasoned outdoorsman, like your brother, could've gotten lost," said the sheriff. "I've likely been sheriff longer than you've been alive, Ms. Baker. In my experience, in cases like this, there's alcohol involved. And if your brother'd been drinking…" His voice trailed off, but she heard the implication loud and clear.

She couldn't deny that the sheriff's explanation was plausible. Sure, it had been years since the last time her brother drank. But, more than once, Axl had sworn off drinking, then fallen back into old habits. Was the explanation really so simple? She wasn't sure, but Everly refused to give up on her brother so easily.

"Have you searched for his camera?" she asked.

"Until now, I didn't know to look for one."

"Well, you should see what you can find."

Sheriff Haak gave an exasperated sigh. "Ms. Baker, why don't you let me do my job?"

Biting off what she really wanted to say, Everly clenched her teeth until her jaw ached. This man wasn't going to be any help, she could tell. That meant it was up to Everly to discover the truth. "Then if you can point me in the direction of where my brother's body was found, I'll look myself."

"Can't do that."

The hollow nothingness of grief was slowly replaced with a seething fury. She managed to keep her voice calm and steady. "Why not?"

"First, you could contaminate the scene," he said. "But there's more. Your brother was found on private property. You'd need the owner's permission to go traipsing around his land. He was the one who found Axl Baker, by the way, and called in the report."

Jaw still tight, she asked, "Can you introduce me to the owner of the property?"

"Don't need to. You've met him already."

Before Everly could ask what in the world the sheriff meant, he said. "Wyatt Thornton—he's the man who almost knocked you ass-over-teakettle at the door."

Not bothering with a goodbye, Everly rose to her feet and rushed into the corridor. She knew it was probably a bad idea to blow off the sheriff like this, but she refused to miss a chance at finding Wyatt Thornton and learning everything he knew.

But where had he gone?

She pushed out the front door and stood in the bitter cold. Luckily, Wyatt Thornton was tall, and therefore easy to find. He stood on the opposite side of the square with a large tank of propane in each hand. He began to cross the street and she rushed after him.

"Mr. Thornton," she called. "Mr. Thornton, can I speak to you for a minute!"

His pace increased.

She ran after him, her lungs burning with the thin mountain air.

He stopped next to a blue pickup truck and set the tanks in the rear bed, before strapping them in place. He removed a set of keys from his pocket.

"Mr. Thornton," she said as she advanced, her breath ragged. "That is you, right? I need your help."

Without a word, he opened the door. "I thought you said you didn't want my assistance."

So that's how he was going to act? Childish? Everly swallowed down the sharpest edges of her anger. "Look, I'm sorry if I was rude before. But I need to speak to you. It's important, Mr. Thornton."

"Wyatt," he said.

"What?"

"Call me Wyatt."

"Okay, Wyatt, I just need a few minutes of your time."

He didn't ask what she needed, but neither did he

walk away, so Everly continued. "The sheriff told me that you found my brother's body yesterday. I'd like to ask you a few questions."

Nothing.

Repeating what she'd told the sheriff, she said, "My brother was a wildlife photographer. If he was out in the middle of the night, it was for a reason—likely some assignment or other. Did you find his camera?"

Shaking his head, Wyatt said, "I didn't, but I didn't know to look for one, either."

It was the same thing the sheriff had told her. "If I could just get your permission and some directions, I could take a look. I won't be a bother, I promise."

"Sorry, but no."

"No?" she asked, her voice reedy. "Why not?"

"I told the sheriff everything. The investigation's up to him."

"I just want to see where you found his body. It might help me understand what happened. He was my brother, my only family." She paused, hating that she had shared more than she intended—hating even more that she was about to beg. "I really need answers. Please."

For a long moment, Wyatt said nothing. Everly could sense the war raging in his mind, see the furrows between his brow, his jaw flex.

"Please," she whispered again.

"I'm sorry," he said at last. "I can't get involved, and letting you come out to my place won't bring your brother back."

"What am I supposed to do?"

Wyatt looked at the ground as he scraped his toe on the cracked sidewalk. "The medical examiner's report will be in later today or tomorrow. After that, you'll have the answers you need."

Another thought came to Everly—Wyatt Thornton was hiding something. To hell with being polite—she was done. "What aren't you telling me?"

"The mountains are a hard place to survive, even with training. Accidents happen. The death of your brother is a monumental life event and you want it to have a greater meaning than just…he simply ran into bad luck." He met her gaze. "But sometimes that's all you have—a lousy destiny. I hope the autopsy gives you the answers you need."

"And if it doesn't?"

"Go home, anyway. There's nothing here for you," he said, not without sympathy.

With that, Wyatt Thornton got behind the wheel. She remained rooted to the spot as he started the engine and backed up. She watched as he drove down the main road and out of town.

He wanted her to go home—give up was more like it. Well, if he thought that she was going to be that easy to get rid of, Wyatt Thornton had better think again.

Chapter 2

Everly parked in front of the Pleasant Pines Inn, a sprawling late 19th century building of stone and timber that overlooked the town. It was the only hotel for miles and while it wasn't a five-star property on Michigan Avenue, it had loads of charm and would suit her needs nicely.

Trailing her suitcase behind her, she approached the front desk. A tall and muscular woman, with her blond hair pulled into a tight bun, greeted Everly with a smile. "May I help you?"

"I need a room," said Everly, stating the obvious.

"Reservations?" the woman asked.

In her haste to get out of Chicago, Everly hadn't bothered with the online registration. "No," Everly said. "I hope you have something available." If not, she'd have to make the three hour commute from Cheyenne.

The desk clerk tapped on a computer keyboard. "You're in luck. We have one room available, second floor. There's also a pub on-site along with a restaurant that serves dinner and breakfast. Both open today at five o'clock." She pointed in the direction of the establishments as she spoke. "What brings you to Pleasant Pines?"

Without question, the clerk was the most helpful person she'd met in Pleasant Pines. Everly read her name tag. "Darcy, can you tell me if Axl Baker had a room here?"

The desk clerk looked over her shoulder before answering in a low voice. "He did…but Mr. Baker's room is off-limits by the order of Sheriff Haak."

At least Everly knew for certain that her brother had been at this hotel. The question was, how could she get the sheriff to let her search her brother's room? Or rather, she knew that answer—he wouldn't. What she needed was a way, legal or not, to get inside the room.

She didn't have much time to plan, so her strategy was simple. Yet, it might just work.

Coughing, Everly touched her throat. "Any chance I can get a bottle of water?"

Darcy held up one finger. "Just a second, I can grab you one from the back."

Heart racing, Everly waited until the other woman disappeared through a doorway. On tiptoe, she looked over the edge of the counter. Papers. Pens.

A computer keyboard. She lifted a pile of papers and it fell out. It was the size and shape of a credit card with two stylized pine trees intertwined with the words *Pleasant Pines* in gilt script. Written in marker were four other words, the ones she needed to see: *Front desk. Total access.*

She'd found a passkey. *Score.*

She didn't hesitate and slipped the keycard into the palm of her hand. She put the papers on the desk and stepped back just as Darcy returned.

"Here you go," she said, holding out the water.

Everly took the bottle awkwardly with her left hand. "Thanks," she said, slipping her right hand into her pocket, where she deposited the stolen card.

Reaching for the handle of her suitcase, she turned from the front desk. How many rooms did this inn have and, more important, how would she find out which one had been her brother's?

"Ms. Baker?" Darcy called.

Everly increased her pace, as if she could outrun the awful truth that she had stolen a key to every door in the hotel.

"Ms. Baker? Ms. Baker?"

Damn, she'd been caught. Everly tried to think of an excuse. Nothing came to mind. Her mouth went dry. She stopped and turned around. "Yes?"

"You forgot your key." Darcy held up a keycard, a twin to the one she had in her pocket, save for the note in marker. "Room two twenty-three. Second floor. The elevator is at the end of the hallway."

Everly swayed as her knees went weak. She was

determined to find out what really happened to her brother, a few rules be damned. And yet, she was hardly used to a life of crime. What she was used to—and quite good at—was public relations, which meant knowing her customer. If her read on Darcy was right, the other woman was likely to be helpful and sympathetic.

"Thanks," she said again. Then she asked, "Do you happen to remember Axl Baker? He's my brother. He *was* my brother." Everly's voice cracked on the last word.

Darcy lowered her eyes. "I heard what happened. I'm so sorry, hon." She lifted her gaze to Everly's. "I wasn't at work when he checked in, but he did come through the lobby on his way to and from the pub."

The pub. Had Axl decided to have a beer? Or more? It wouldn't have been the first time he thought that he could handle a little alcohol and been wrong. Hadn't she worried that eventually out-of-control drinking would be the death of him? More than that, the sheriff had all but predicted that drinking was involved in the accidental death.

That was, if Axl's death was an accident. "Any idea what he was doing?"

"I'm not sure," said Darcy with a shake of her head. "He wasn't there long—thirty minutes or so." She paused and bit her bottom lip. "The bartender comes in at four o'clock—she might remember something."

Everly checked her phone for the time. 12:04 p.m. What might Everly discover in the next three and a half hours?

Did it really matter in light of the fact that Axl was gone? Was what Wyatt Thornton had said been true? Did Everly want a monumental explanation for a simple set of facts? No. She owed her brother the truth and she'd never forgive herself if she didn't find out what happened.

"Oh, if you could talk to the bartender and see what she remembers I would so appreciate it," said Everly with a small smile. "You'd be the first person actually trying to help me around here."

Turning, she wheeled her luggage down the main corridor. There were a dozen rooms on the first floor, and she guessed there were twice as many on the second. A deep green runner stretched the entire length of the hallway, with identical doors on each side. Brass numbers were affixed to each door, along with a keycard entry.

Since she had no idea which room had belonged to her brother, Everly decided a room-by-room search was in order. She also decided to start on the second floor, when something caught her eye. A paper tag had been placed over one of the locks. *Do Not Disturb* had been preprinted on the label. But it was the printed memo from the Pleasant Pines sheriff's office on the door that caught her attention:

No entry by order of the Sheriff's Department.

Bingo.

Everly didn't want to wait another minute to get into her brother's room. Looking over her shoulder, she found that the corridor was empty. After fishing the passkey from her pocket, she opened the door. Even before she stepped into the room, she knew she'd found the right place. It smelled like Axl. It was a combination of grass and dirt. No matter the occasion, Axl always smelled like the outdoors. Yet, to smell it now was both cruel and beautiful. She bit the inside of her lip hard enough to staunch a new flood of tears.

To Everly, it looked like the sheriff's deputies had already gone through the place. All the clothes had been taken from the suitcase and were piled haphazardly on one of the beds—something Axl wouldn't do. Likewise, the closet doors were open, his jackets thrown next to the pile.

A fine gray powder covered the dresser. The nightstand. Even the TV remote. It must be fingerprint powder.

For a moment, she wondered about all the crime shows she'd ever watched on TV. Was she contaminating the room, with her fingerprints or hair, just by being here? Then again what she needed were facts about what happened if she wanted to get the sheriff to look into Axl's death.

Setting aside her suitcase, she left the door slightly ajar. The curtains had been drawn and only a sliver of light shone through the place where the seams did not meet. In the dim light, she scanned the nondescript hotel room. A bureau with a TV stood against one wall. A mirror hung just to the left. A desk was next to the bureau. A chair and small table took up a corner.

There were also two beds. Both were made, but one had an opened suitcase and a shaving kit piled on it, but no camera. She riffled through the suitcase and patted down the pile of his clothes. In the pocket of a fleece jacket, she found Axl's cell phone.

Alarm bells began ringing in her mind. Like the camera, Axl was never without his phone. Everly picked it up and pressed the home button. At one time her thumbprint had been programmed into the phone. But was it still?

Holding her breath, she waited.

The home screen appeared. She scrolled through the texts—all from his work. There were no voice mails. She checked his calendar...and found one entry.

9:00 p.m. March 21. Meet at bar.

So, he had gone to the bar to meet someone. But who? More than that, was the sheriff right? Had her brother been drunk and foolish?

Everly heard the whisper of a sound and turned. As her gaze passed over the mirror, she caught a fleeting glimpse of a shadowy form. Blood froze in her veins and she began to scream. The sound died in her throat as a sharp pain filled her skull. Everly stumbled, her legs no longer able to hold her upright.

And then she pitched forward, falling into a pool of blackness.

* * *

The engine revved as it climbed the hill. The wrought iron gate that led to Wyatt's property stood open and inviting. In the distance, he saw the wide porch of his refurbished farmhouse. The newly installed solar panels winked in the early afternoon light. Pressing down on the accelerator, he rocketed past the driveway, cursing himself for what he was about to do.

Three years ago, Wyatt walked away from the FBI, after realizing he could no longer trust his instincts. So why was he now returning to the place where Axl Baker's body had been found? Did he not have any confidence in the sheriff? Had Baker's sister goaded him into looking for something that may not exist?

Or was it what he feared—that the similarities to his final case proved that he was *still* stuck in the past after all this time?

Wyatt didn't like any of the possibilities.

Nothing that happened was really any of Wyatt's business. Yet, he couldn't let it go.

It was almost twelve fifteen when the turnoff for the old schoolhouse came into view. Pulling onto the shoulder, Wyatt turned off the ignition. With a final curse, he leaped from the truck. Wind whipped off the mountains and howled as it danced along the plain. Shoving his hands into the pockets of his vest, he walked slowly to the rutted track.

He kneeled next to a sapling. The little tree was hardly higher than ten inches, and yet it had been snapped in half. Wyatt recalled the sheriff clambering out of his large truck, the undercarriage more than a foot off the ground. There was no way that the big truck had broken the little tree.

If not Haak's vehicle, then what had?

On foot, Wyatt followed the path. It was as if every plant that grew above four inches had been mowed down. Definitely done by the grille of something low—most likely a sedan. Was it a clue to a mystery, or simply an oddity with a reasonable explanation?

Clouds roiled at the peaks of the Rockies, promising to bring cold, wind and more snow. In less than ten minutes, he'd covered the last half of a mile and the little schoolhouse came into view.

The first thing he noticed was that the stench of death was gone—once the body had been taken away, no doubt the structure had been able to air out. Yellow-and-black police tape had been stretched across the door, barring entry. But it was more of a warning than a true obstacle and Wyatt ducked underneath to enter the single room. Without the body, the space seemed bigger and brighter. Less ominous.

Wyatt spent a minute trying to imagine the room in a bygone era, with a score of children sitting obediently behind rows of wooden desks. The image never held, and his mind returned to what he had seen yesterday. The body. Stone and wood. Sunlight and shadow.

A gust of wind shook the walls and sent a leaf

skittering across the floor. Bit by bit, the natural world was laying claim to the structure. He kneeled and picked up the leaf, twisting it between his fingers. Yesterday the floor had been clean, and now not.

There had to be something that he'd missed.

Thinking back to Everly Baker's insistence about her brother's habits, Wyatt stepped back outside, scanning the ground around the cabin for any sign of Axl's missing camera. The glint of metal. Glass, reflecting the light.

There was nothing.

With his back to the door, Wyatt crossed his arms over his chest and looked across the horizon. The mountains. The plains. The sky. And him alone in the world, just like he wanted.

Still, the mystery of Axl Baker's death was now, uncomfortably, a part of him, like dirt tattooed into the creases of his knuckles. The unanswered questions lingered, pinging away at him like popcorn in a hot pan. A body with no evident cause of death. No signs that the deceased had struggled, either. The floor, that yesterday was swept clean. Plants, broken on the trail. The missing camera. The sister, desperate for answers.

Each was a piece to a puzzle. But in reality— together, did they create a picture? Or were they even connected in the first place?

Was the broken vegetation a clue? Not really, especially when Wyatt considered that the medical examiner would've followed the same path when he came to collect the body. The dirt-free floor was harder to explain but wasn't impossible.

But what about Everly Baker? He had the power to help her. What had he offered? Nothing but trite advice. Definitely not his finest hour.

He spoke her name out loud. "Everly Baker." The wind stole the words before he could decide if he liked the way they tasted.

The feeling of their accidental touch lingered on his fingertips. Her skin had been soft, and a sweetly spicy scent surrounded her. It was somehow homey and sexy at the same time. Her eyes, a jade green, had spoken of sadness and strength.

He rubbed his fingers on his jeans.

But it had been there, something he hadn't felt—or wanted to feel—for such a long time. It was a connection with another person.

He'd come to Wyoming three years before to escape. Escape the scrutiny of higher-ups. Escape all of the questions from the media. Escape the stress, and, most important, escape the doubts that constantly nagged him, even in his dreams.

No. He wouldn't get involved in the unexplained death. He'd left the need to hunt down killers in his past life—that was, if Axl Baker hadn't died of natural causes. A few stray snowflakes danced on the wind. He looked at the mountains and the peak was gone—completely obscured by the clouds. Soon enough, the storm would be in the valley and Wyatt didn't want to be caught lingering by the old schoolhouse.

Turning back to the track, Wyatt began the walk to his waiting truck. From there, he'd take the road home and return to the life that kept him safe. Sheltered.

Alone.

Everly was swimming. The water was dark and cold. The surface hovered above her, just out of reach. A voice called to her from the shore.

"Ms. Baker? Ms. Baker? Can you hear me?"

Everly wanted to speak, but her mouth filled with murky water. Gasping, she broke the surface and found that she was lying on a carpeted floor. She could feel a rough mark imprinted on her cheek, yet nothing else seemed real.

"Ms. Baker?" A tall blond woman was kneeling next to Everly.

And then it all came back to her—Axl's death, his missing camera, her stealing the keycard to get into his room. But why was she on the floor?

"Ms. Baker, can you hear me?" It was the woman who worked at the front desk and her name was Darcy; she now remembered that, too.

"What happened?" Everly's mouth was dry, her lip was tender.

"I came down the hall and saw that the door was opened a bit. I thought maybe one of the deputies had come by. I almost closed it without looking, but I peeked in and saw you on the floor."

Everly sat up—the back of her head throbbed. She glanced at the bedside clock. She'd only been out for a few minutes. "I was hit," she said, recalling the single glimpse of the silhouette in the mirror.

"Hit?" echoed Darcy. Her voice was a whisper. "By who?"

"I didn't see a face," said Everly. "Just a shadow."

"Are you sure? There wasn't anyone in the hall. Nobody came through the lobby, either."

"Well, I know what I saw, and I know what happened to me," Everly insisted.

"You wait here," said Darcy as she got to her feet. "I'm going to call Sheriff Haak, and the doctor, too. A hit to the head that's strong enough to knock you out probably gave you a concussion."

The sheriff? So far Darcy hadn't pressed Everly for how she got into the room, even though it was obvious. What would the sheriff say? Certainly, Everly had broken at least one law when she stole the keycard and entered a room that wasn't hers—the official order to stay out notwithstanding.

Then again, Everly would bet anything that the attack hadn't been random. She'd been targeted. That didn't put anyone else at risk, but it left *her* exposed. The bump on the back of her head was a warning—nothing more. If anyone wanted her dead, they could've easily killed her in the minutes that she was unconscious. The thought left her chilled, and she crossed her arms over her chest to staunch a tremble.

"Hold on a second," she called to Darcy. Everly stood slowly, the throbbing at the back of her head increasing in tempo and intensity. "I'm not sure that

I was hit. I mean, I hit the back of my head—but I might have fainted and come down on the edge of the nightstand."

"You were so sure you'd been attacked just a minute ago."

"My brother died unexpectedly, and I flew all night from Chicago to be here. I was standing in his room and it smells like he did, you know. It was overwhelming." Everly sighed and touched the lump on the back of her head. She winced. "To be honest, there's nothing that I'm actually sure of right now."

"Even if you don't know, you should still talk to the sheriff."

"I really don't want him involved."

Darcy shook her head. "You have been through a lot and I don't want to make trouble for you. Just, please, don't make any more trouble for yourself. Sheriff Haak is a good man—he'll figure out what happened."

"I hope so," said Everly.

"If you fell, you still need to see a doctor. I can call him for you."

"I've met Doc Lambert already. I'll get in touch once I get to my room," said Everly, even though she had no intention of calling anyone.

"Are you sure?" asked Darcy.

As if to prove that she was fit, Everly grabbed the handle of her suitcase and rolled it from the room. "Positive," she said, then added, "Thanks for everything."

Darcy followed Everly and pulled the door closed.

"Call the front desk if you need anything at all— that's legal at least."

Everly held out the purloined keycard. "Sorry about that," she said.

Darcy took the card. "Just don't do it again, and we'll be even."

After giving the desk clerk a wave, she walked to the elevator. Thank goodness Everly knew how to sell a story. In fact, her bit about fainting had been so convincing that Everly almost believed it herself. Now that she didn't have to deal with the sheriff, she needed to find out who would want to keep her away from Axl's death.

In her estimation, there was only one suspect. It was the same man who wanted her gone and had also found her brother's body.

Everly wheeled the luggage to her room and entered. Despite the fact that her head still throbbed, she sat at the desk. Removing her laptop, she powered it up and entered two words into the search engine. Wyatt Thornton.

There wasn't much on the internet about Wyatt Thornton. A real-estate transaction, along with a local address. She wrote down the address. And a notice that he'd adopted a dog from a county rescue.

There had to be more. In this day and age, nobody lived off the grid. And if they did, it was because they didn't want to be found.

She tried again. W. Thornton.

The search was met with a question. *Did you mean Special Agent W. Thornton?* Thousands of hits followed. She scanned headlines from articles about a notorious serial killer in Las Vegas and the FBI profiler in charge of the case: W. Thornton. She moved the cursor to hover over the *No* icon. Then she stopped. Her eye was drawn to a photograph of several FBI agents, and one of them was unquestionably the same one she met earlier today, Wyatt Thornton.

His hair was longer now, with just a touch of gray that he hadn't had when the photo had been taken years ago. The suit he wore had been replaced with jeans, but it was him.

Immediately she wondered why he'd come to Wyoming and, more important, why not tell Everly if he had a professional opinion about her brother's death?

She clicked on the article, which was four years old. A string of killings—all single men—had stunned the hard-to-shock city of Las Vegas. The FBI, through their behavioral scientist, Thornton, had a suspect. On closer scrutiny, the suspect had an alibi for one of the killings. It was a fact that had been missed, or possibly suppressed, by Thornton.

The media didn't have a killer, but they had an incompetent or possibly dishonest FBI agent. Thornton had been crucified by the press. And the killings? They stopped. One subsequent article wondered if it hadn't been a fabrication of Thornton's all along.

For a moment, she felt sorry for Wyatt. And then she wondered—if he'd have come to her for public-relations help, what would she have said? Probably that he should move someplace where no one knew who he was, or didn't care.

At least she knew what he'd been trying to hide and why he wanted no part of a possible murder investigation.

She hesitated for only a minute before pushing back from the desk. She grabbed the keys to her rental car. As she picked up the hastily copied address, she made a decision. Wyatt Thornton had investigated murders before. He was an expert in unexplained crimes. He would know how to put all the puzzle pieces together and his was an expertise she was determined to use.

Chapter 3

Wyatt sat behind his desk and stared at the computer screen. Nearby, a fire crackled in the hearth. Gus was lying in the middle of the room, soaking up the warmth. Eyes closed, the dog's chest rose and fell with each breath.

Call it a compulsion, but despite vowing that he'd leave the Axl Baker investigation alone, Wyatt had dug an old case file from where he stored his important paperwork in the spare bedroom. He'd also opened an internet search for the deceased. So far, there was nothing of interest. Criminal record: two DUIs along with one violation of the Illinois open-container law. All three incidents had occurred more than seven years ago.

Wyatt also found a testimonial from Axl detailing his time in a Chicago addiction treatment center, along with several of his photographs that were part of an auction held five years back. Since that time, there'd been nothing.

Professionally, Baker was a successful photographer who worked freelance for some of the world's most popular nature magazines. Just as his sister had said, he had plenty of experience to survive a night or two outside in the wilderness. Could it be suicide? It was impossible to really know anyone. Still, taking his own life didn't seem to fit the profile here.

Gus lifted his head and looked toward the window, letting out a bark.

He heard the engine a moment before he saw the car's light cutting through the gathering storm. A car turned from the main road onto his driveway. The promised snow had arrived, and the car's headlights illuminated the flakes as they fell.

Standing at the window, Wyatt peered into the storm. Gus moved to his side and lifted his paws to the sill, barking as the car pulled up to the house.

"I see her, boy." Even from a distance, he could see the driver—Everly Baker. The feeling of her hand beneath his fingertips returned. The memory ran up his arm and traveled down his spine. With a shiver, he threw another log on the fire.

Gus began to bark in earnest and Wyatt saved the internet search for Axl Baker, then powered down his computer. The doorbell chimed, and he paused a moment. Everly Baker was the first visitor to his house and Wyatt's jaw instinctively tightened.

He glanced around the room—sofa, desk, easy chair. TV on the wall. Exposed wooden beams on the ceiling. He'd done all the work to the house himself, knocking down walls to create a single room. More that, Wyatt had kept the original moldings and window seat. Through all his time and effort he had created more than a home—a refuge.

Yet, he hadn't dedicated years to have his house invaded by an uninvited guest.

He opened the door and there she was, on his stoop, hand lifted and ready to knock. The wind whipped through her hair, making it look like she was surrounded by flames. She was more than beautiful, she was fierce—the vengeful goddess of a Celtic clan. Then he reminded himself that her problem was not his and he decided to be as unfriendly as possible. "What do you want?"

Gus nosed past Wyatt, his tail wagging. The dog approached Everly, panting.

She bent down and ran her hands through the dog's coat. "Well, who's a handsome boy?"

The dog licked Everly's chin. So much for being unfriendly. She giggled.

"Gus, come here."

His order went ignored.

"Gus," he said, dropping his voice.

The dog looked over his shoulder and trotted to stand at Wyatt's side.

"Sweet dog," said Everly, rising to her feet.

Wyatt shrugged. "You didn't come here to meet my dog. What do you want?"

"Aren't you going to invite me in?"

"I wasn't planning on it," he said.

"It's freezing out here and I just want to talk to you for a minute." She blew on her hands and rubbed them together. "I bet Gus has a warm belly that he likes to have rubbed."

The dog barked excitedly. Wyatt opened the door. "You can have a minute but leave my dog's belly alone."

After leading her to the den, he gestured to the sofa. "Have a seat."

She sat as he took a chair opposite her. She slipped out of her coat and Wyatt took a moment to admire her outfit and the way it molded to her curves. A long, cream colored sweater accentuated her breasts and a pair of leggings skimmed over her long legs. Despite the simplicity of her outfit, Everly Baker was chic and totally out of place in his modified farmhouse.

"I won't waste your time with small talk," she began. "I need your help."

"Lady," he said. "I'm the wrong person to come to for help."

She ignored his statement and continued to speak. "There's something wrong regarding my brother's death and I don't know what it is. I get the feeling the sheriff wants this all to go away quickly and aside from him, there's no one I can trust." Everly paused, then said, "Except you."

"What makes you think I'm trustworthy?"

Gus wandered to the sofa and placed his head on Everly's lap.

Traitor.

"I did a little Googling." She stroked the top of Gus's head and continued, as if talking to the dog. "It wasn't like the information was hard to find. I know who you are, Special Agent Thornton. More than that, I know that you can help me figure out what happened to my brother."

Wyatt hadn't been called Special Agent for years. Nor did he ever want to hear his old title spoken again. His insides turned cold and hard. "You really should leave."

"The press didn't treat you fairly," Everly continued as if he hadn't just ordered her from his home. "I mean, it's their job to sell papers and get viewers— but I don't think you did anything wrong."

Who was she to decide how he'd been treated? She wasn't there. She didn't know what it was to have his life ruined by innuendo and implications. Rising to his feet, he pointed to the door. "Out," he said.

Everly lifted her palms. "Like I said, I'm trying to figure out what's going on. I need an expert and you're an expert. I need you. I can pay, if that's the problem. Just name your price."

"My past is none of your business and I'm definitely not interested in your money." His pulse raced, pounding in his skull. Clenching his teeth, Wyatt said, "Get the hell out of my house and don't ever come back."

Gus whimpered and slunk to his bed in the corner.

Everly stood. All the color drained from her cheeks, leaving her chalky. She drew in a deep breath. It didn't do much for her complexion. "I didn't mean to invade your privacy."

Snorting, Wyatt said, "You're kidding, right? You look me up on the internet, find out all my dirty secrets, get my address and then come to my house uninvited? The only thing you've done is invade my privacy."

With a nod, Everly turned to go. She picked up her coat from the sofa and slid it over her shoulders. "You're right," she said. "I didn't care anything about your privacy, but I need to know what happened to my brother. I snuck into his hotel room and was attacked. That's why I found you on the internet—"

"Attacked?" Wyatt interrupted. "By whom?"

With a shake of her head, Everly said, "They came up from behind and hit me hard enough to knock me out. When I found out who you are—were—I knew I had to ask for help. I'm sorry to have bothered you."

"What did the sheriff say about the attack?" Wyatt really had to stop acting like he cared. Someone might get the wrong idea.

Everly regarded him for a moment. Her eyes were ringed with dark circles. She didn't just look tired, she looked exhausted. "I imagine Sheriff Haak would be more upset that I broke into Axl's room than that I'd been assaulted."

"I'm sure you know that you shouldn't be driving if you'd lost consciousness."

"I was healthy enough to drive out here, wasn't I?"

"No offense, but you look like crap."

"Gee, thanks."

"You just look like you've had a rough day, that's all."

"The worst of my life," she said. Her eyes shone with tears and she looked away.

Wyatt hesitated. Against his better judgment, he could feel his resolve softening slightly. "If you looked me up on the internet, then you can guess why I don't want to get involved in any suspicious deaths."

"You think there's something to investigate?"

"I didn't say that," Wyatt retorted. "I meant that there's no immediate medical reason for your brother to have died."

"Axl was found on your property, right? You can take me there now and show me where you found him, at least. Maybe we can find his camera. It wasn't in his room, which means it's still out there, somewhere. There's got to be a link or a clue."

Wyatt refused to admit that she was right. He also refused to admit that he'd already looked for the camera but found nothing. He turned to the floor-to-ceiling windows and saw nothing but the whiteness of the swirling snow. "There's no real road out to the old schoolhouse, just a rutted track. With weather like this, it'd be easy to get disoriented or stranded. So, I'm not going out there until the weather clears, and neither are you." He exhaled, realizing that he was about to make the worst decision of his entire life. "I'll give you a ride back to town while the roads are clear, though. You shouldn't be driving with a head injury and in a storm, no less." He held up a hand to stop her protest. "And, I'll agree to review all the facts and evidence that we have so far. If there's something that doesn't seem right about your brother, I'll talk to Sheriff Haak personally."

Back in Pleasant Pines, Everly stood on the sidewalk in front of a restaurant. The wind was turning the snow into projectiles that left the skin on her face raw. The lump at the back of her head thumped with each beat of her heart. "Pie?" she said, echoing Wyatt's last word.

"Yeah, pie. Flaky crust. Filling of choice."

A lock of hair blew across her face and she pulled it away. "Why pie?"

Wyatt lifted one shoulder and let it drop. "I like pie," he said. "It's like a ritual. Helps me think." Pulling open the glass door, he gestured for her to enter. "Come on. Let's get out of the cold."

Everly stepped into Sally's on Main. Half a dozen booths lined the wall by the door. Opposite was a counter with stools and in between sat several small tables. Aside from another couple in the back booth and a woman behind the counter, the restaurant was empty.

Wyatt slid into a booth halfway back and Everly took the opposite seat. The woman from behind the counter approached with a pen and order pad in hand.

"Hey, sugar," the older woman said to Wyatt. "What can I get for you?"

"Got some apple pie, Sally?"

"Sure do," she said. "You want that warmed and served with ice cream?"

"Is there any other way?" asked Wyatt. "And a cup of coffee."

Sally turned to Everly. "What about you, hon?"

"I'd love some apple pie, thanks."

The couple from the back of the restaurant stood and walked forward. The man, tall with a shaved head, nodded a greeting at Everly, then glanced at Wyatt and stopped abruptly. "Wyatt? Wyatt Thornton? I haven't seen you in forever."

"Marcus?" Wyatt got to his feet and shook the other man's hand. "Marcus Jones, it's great to see you. What're you doing in Pleasant Pines?"

"I'm grabbing a late lunch with my friend Chloe Ryder. She's the local district attorney." He whistled through his teeth. "I honestly never thought I'd see you again. You disappeared after leaving the Bureau. What are you doing with yourself these days?"

"I live in Pleasant Pines."

"Well, it's great to see you. Wyatt, this is Chloe. Chloe, Wyatt."

Chloe, a tall brunette with a fringe of bangs, took Wyatt's hand. "It's a pleasure," she said with a smile.

"Nice to meet you, Chloe," Wyatt said. "Ah, this is Everly Baker." He paused, and she wondered how he was going to explain her to the duo. "She's from Chicago."

Pleasantries were exchanged and then Wyatt

asked, "How's work? Are you still the special agent in charge in the Denver office?"

"I left the Bureau, if you can believe that."

"Been there, done that, have the T-shirt."

Marcus laughed. "Anyway, I joined a private security group out of Denver and we've opened an office in Wyoming. What about you? Where are you working now?"

"Me?" Wyatt shook his head. "I quit altogether after what happened in Las Vegas. A quiet life suits me just fine."

"Maybe you should stop by. You could be a great asset to the team."

"I'm not much into being a team player anymore," said Wyatt.

"You never know. Private security might suit you better than a quiet life."

"Private security," Wyatt repeated. "What does that mean? Are you a private investigator? Do you find cheating spouses?"

"We are so much more than that." He took a pad of paper and a pen from his coat pocket and scribbled for a moment. "That's my cell number. Call and I'll give you the tour—tell you a few war stories. Hell, some of them might even be true."

"I'm not interested in work, but thanks." Wyatt waved away the offered paper.

"Take it," said Marcus. "You never know when you might need a friend."

Wyatt folded the sheet of paper placing it in his back pocket.

"Anyway," said Marcus, "Chloe has to get back to work, and I'll let you two get back to your date."

Date. The one word hung in the air, like smoke. It reminded Everly of how handsome Wyatt Thornton was and how very long it had been since she'd actually gone out on a date. "He seems nice," said Everly once they were alone.

"Marcus Jones is as good as they come."

Sally returned with their pie and coffee. The conversation stalled as she set everything on the table. Everly took a bite, chewing slowly. The crust was light and buttery, the apples inside sweet, with just a touch of spice. She sighed. "You're right," she said. "Best pie ever."

Wyatt smiled. "I'm glad you like it, but let's get back to why we're here to begin with. First, do you know what your brother was supposed to photograph?"

"A wolf-pack migration, I think," she said. She bit her lip. "I can't recall the magazine he was on assignment for, but I can find out."

"Do you think he was targeted because of his work?"

She took a sip of coffee, which was surprisingly good for a diner in Nowheresville, USA. "No way. My brother was a good person and could charm the hell out of anyone. And he was good at what he did, the best photographer I've seen. Everyone loved Axl."

Wyatt scooped a bite of pie into his mouth. "What else?"

Everly's mind had been so full of possibilities, but now it was empty. Then she remembered. "The sheriff gave me a list of all Axl's possessions." She dug through her purse and found the folded note.

Flattening the sheet on the table, she read aloud. "Shirt, shoes, socks, wallet, three credit cards in the name of Axl James Baker. One hundred and twenty dollars in twenty-dollar bills and half of a two-dollar bill."

"Wait," said Wyatt. "Go back. Read the last line again, the one about the money."

"One hundred and twenty dollars in twenty-dollar bills and half of a two-dollar bill."

"The last case I worked." He paused.

"The serial killer in Las Vegas," Everly offered.

"He left a calling card of sorts on each of the victims. To avoid copycat killers, we never shared that fact with the media." Wyatt paused and took a drink of coffee. "It was half of a two-dollar bill."

Everly began to tremble. She grasped her hands together and asked with a whisper, "Are you saying…? Did a serial killer murder my brother?"

"It's worse than that," said Wyatt.

Everly couldn't imagine what might be worse. "Really? How is that possible?"

"Not only was your brother murdered, but the killer is on the loose in Pleasant Pines. As that bump on your head proves, he knows exactly who you are—and you could very well be the next victim."

The stench of antiseptic hung in the air and Carl Haak's eyes watered. He leaned against the stainless steel counter and concentrated on the feeling of cold metal against his hip. The corpse of Axl Baker was laid out on a table, a cloth pulled up to his chest.

"My initial finding," said Doctor Lambert, "is that the deceased had a blood-alcohol content of point-one-five."

"That's good and drunk," said the sheriff, "and well above the legal limit, but not enough to cause death."

Doctor Lambert was a slight man with gray hair and a pointy beard. The combination always put Carl in the mind of a billy goat. Doc Lambert stroked the end of his beard for a moment. "I don't think so, either."

"Then why do we have a corpse?"

"My best guess? Our Mr. Baker drank too much, got lost and either laid down to sleep it off or he passed out in the old schoolhouse. The alcohol would've slowed his circulation, making it easier for hypothermia to set in. He simply never woke up."

"Are you willing to put that as the cause on a death certificate?"

Doctor Lambert stroked his beard again. "There's no other explanation. No other trauma. No bruising anywhere. No signs of cardiac arrest. Nothing." With a nod, he moved to the counter next to Carl and a tablet computer. After typing in a few notes, he said, "I'm calling it. Cause of death is accidental exposure. I'll file the paperwork with the county office and the body will be ready for transport first thing in the morning."

Carl quickly thanked the doctor and pushed open the door. He took in deep, gulping breaths as he strode down the basement hallway. A set of stairs led to the hospital's ground floor. He avoided the main entrance and emergency room, sneaking out a side door instead.

A cold wind hit him in the face and blew away the remaining odor from the morgue. He pulled up the collar of his coat and shouldered his way through the gathering snow. Only two weeks, Carl reminded himself, and he'd be done with the bitter cold. Done with this job. Until then, a few things remained to be done.

He needed to meet with Axl Baker's sister. And he was dreading the conversation.

Figuring she'd have checked into the Pleasant Pines Inn—since it was the only lodging in town—he headed in that direction. Walking down Main Street, he glanced in the window of *Sally's* and stumbled. There, in one of the middle booths, sat Everly Baker along with Wyatt Thornton. No time like the present, he thought, so he pushed open the door and entered the restaurant.

Everly looked up and Carl lifted a hand in greeting. As he approached the booth, he said, "I saw you from outside and decided to stop. I hope you don't mind, but I have news."

Wyatt moved over in his seat, making room for Carl. "I'm glad you're here, Sheriff. We have something for you, too."

Carl didn't exactly ignore the comment, but he

didn't want to be distracted. "I just spoke to the medical examiner. It seems your brother had a good bit of alcohol in his system. It decreases circulation and the cold and exposure likely affected his body temperature as well, no matter how good an outdoorsman you tell us he was." He removed his hat, set it on the table and sat. "I'm sorry, Ms. Baker, but your brother's death has been ruled as accidental."

Everly's cheeks reddened. "That's impossible."

"I know this is a shock and not what you'd hoped we'd find." He wasn't sure how to proceed and be delicate at the same time. "I am sorry for your loss."

"It's impossible," she said again. "We have proof that he was murdered."

Carl leaned back in the booth, looking skeptical. "Proof? What kind of proof?"

Wyatt spoke then. "When I was with the FBI, I investigated a string of killings. All the victims were white males and each body was left with half of a two-dollar bill in their pocket or wallet."

"So?"

Wyatt pushed a sheet of paper in front of Carl. The sheriff recognized the list of Axl Baker's belongings. Pointing to a line on the page, Wyatt said, "See…here—a two-dollar bill, and only half of it found with the body."

"And this is your proof? That doesn't mean anything. He could've gotten that money anywhere."

"Tell me if I'm wrong but isn't it odd to find only half a bill?" asked Everly.

"You're wrong," said Carl. "All you have is circumstantial evidence. You're playing guessing games."

"All the victims in Las Vegas had very high blood-alcohol content and had been left for dead."

"Let me get this straight—you're telling me that a murderer was killing people with booze? I've been a police officer for a long time. Too much drink will make you sick long before it'll kill you. It'd be a tough way to murder someone."

"Once we made the connection between the two-dollar bills, we also discovered that the victims had high levels of anti-nausea medicine in their bodies. It was enough to knock them out and let the alcohol poison them."

Carl didn't have anything to counter that claim, not yet at least.

He did have another idea, though. "Well, let's just figure that Axl was killed. Who should I suspect, Wyatt? You? The deceased was found by you on your land, after all. Most of the information I have is from you, too."

"Don't be ridiculous," said Wyatt. "If I killed him, why would I link it to my previous case?"

"It's no more ridiculous than you telling me that there's a serial killer in Pleasant Pines."

"That brings up an interesting point," said Everly. "How many accidental deaths are there in the county each year? How many men go missing while hunting or skiing or hiking in the area?"

Carl poked the table with his finger. "This is my

town. How dare you insinuate that I can't keep my own people safe."

She continued, "I didn't mean to suggest anything, it's just that there's a connection that needs to be explored."

"Your brother's death has been ruled as accidental. End of story. His body will be ready for transport back to Illinois first thing tomorrow. When that happens, I want you gone, Ms. Baker. There's nothing for you to suss out here in Pleasant Pines."

Carl stood and shoved his hat onto his head. He stalked out of the restaurant and into the soft afternoon light.

Chapter 4

Everly gaped at the retreating sheriff. Her shock at the thought that her brother might have been the victim of a serial killer mixed with incredulity over how Sheriff Haak acted. Or was it overreacted? She wanted to scream or cry or throw something. Instead, she just stared after him, numb.

"Tell me that didn't just happen," she said, after a moment.

"It happened."

"I can't believe that Sheriff Haak would dismiss our evidence so quickly."

Wyatt took a sip of his coffee and then scraped up the last bit of pie. He lifted the fork to his mouth and stopped. "He's too territorial for his own good," he said, and then took a bite. After chewing and swallowing, he informed her, "He's retiring soon, and he thinks that having a serial killer in his town would say a lot about the job he's done."

"Well, it would," said Everly.

"I'm not saying he's right or that you're wrong. But I've seen this before—for him it's personal. Then again…" He paused. "It's always that way with cops and a homicide."

It didn't take much for Everly to realize that Wyatt was talking about himself and the case from Las Vegas. "So you're saying that even though there's evidence potentially linking Axl's death to a serial killer, there's nothing I can do, because the sheriff might feel bad? That's the most ridiculous thing I've ever heard."

Wyatt's gaze met hers. "Lower your voice," he whispered.

Everly didn't realize that she'd been yelling, and in truth she really didn't care. All the same, she cast a glance toward the counter and found it empty. Most likely, Sally was in the kitchen. "It doesn't matter how loud I am, or what tone I use," she said, matching Wyatt's whisper with a hiss of her own. "My brother is dead, and the sheriff is willing to sweep all the evidence under the rug."

Wyatt looked outside, his reflection trapped in the window. "I'm in." Turning, he met her gaze. "I'll help you figure out what happened to your brother."

"Are you sure?"

"Do you want my help or not?"

"Of course. It's just…until now, you were just so certain that you wanted nothing to do with this case."

Wyatt sighed. "This is my mess that I failed to clean up in Las Vegas."

"I just want justice for Axl."

Wyatt picked up his cup and took a long drink. "You'll get it, but first we have to keep you safe. Since the killer knows you're in town, you can't keep staying at the Pleasant Pines Inn. Especially since someone already attacked you there."

"It's the only hotel in town. What am I supposed to do? Sleep in my rental car?" Everly asked. At the same time, she knew Wyatt was right. She couldn't stay in the hotel—not alone and with a murderer on the loose.

"I was thinking," said Wyatt. He lifted his eyes to hers.

His eyes were more than brown—there was dark gray woven in, as well. It reminded her of the sky as a storm rolled in from Lake Michigan. He had a cleft in his chin that she hadn't noticed before. She reached for her fork and twirled it through her fingers.

"I was thinking," he repeated. "You could stay at my place."

"I could?" Dear God, had she just squeaked? Clearing her throat, she tried again. "It's a nice offer, but I'm not sure I should accept."

"The way I see it, you really don't have a choice. Besides, this is for your own protection."

Everly felt drawn to Wyatt even more. She'd seen how isolated he was—rather than warning her off, there was something almost…alluring, about him. As if he was a puzzle to be solved.

She'd have to be careful not to become too attached. The reclusive ex-agent wasn't her ideal partner, that's for sure. And yet, there was something undeniably intriguing about him.

"So," she said, "what do we do now?"

"We'll need to get your things from the hotel. Then when we get back to my place, I'll look through my old case file. There might be something in there that can help me."

"Us," she said. "You mean *help us*."

Wyatt rose to his feet and withdrew his wallet from the back pocket of his jeans. He threw several bills on the table. "In all honesty, I work better alone. I always have."

Everly got to her feet, as well. "It's too bad then, because this time you have a partner."

Wyatt pulled into a parking space in front of the Pleasant Pines Inn and turned off the ignition. Was he really going to bring Everly to his house? His home was a sanctuary and to allow another person inside would taint the sacredness of his space. Then again, what he said earlier had been true. She couldn't stay at the hotel, not with a serial killer out there, somewhere. She needed protection.

The question was, did it have to be him?

He gave a passing thought to calling his old buddy from the Bureau, Marcus Jones. A private-security outfit might suit Everly's needs better. But Wyatt knew the real reason he had offered up his house.

He wanted Everly with him.

It was extremely simple and monumentally complicated at the same time.

"I'll be right back," said Everly as she opened the door.

Cold air hit Wyatt in the face, sweeping away the regrets and doubts. He took the keys out of the ignition, shoved them into his pocket and opened his own door. "I'll come with you."

"I'm used to doing things on my own and can handle getting a suitcase by myself," she said with a smile. "I am a big girl, you know."

Wyatt knew all too well that Everly was one-hundred-percent woman. From her long legs, to her fiery tresses, to her full lips, Everly was the complete package. He put aside his attraction and said, "Remember what happened last time?"

She touched the back of her head, her fingers prodding the place where she'd been hit, no doubt. The smile faded. "You're right. Thanks."

They approached the front of the hotel and he pushed open the doors. The desk clerk looked up from her post.

"Hi, Darcy," said Everly. "My plans have changed, and I'll be checking out. Can I get my bill?"

"Since you really didn't use the room there won't be a charge."

"Thanks for everything," said Everly with a smile.

"Ms. Baker," the desk clerk said. "I spoke to the

bartender about the night your brother came into the pub. Do you have a moment?"

Everly sucked in a breath. The color drained from her cheeks, leaving her skin the delicate shade of porcelain. "Of course," she said, still breathless.

"Well, Johanna, that's the bartender, said that she overheard your brother arguing with one of the cooks. His name is Larry Walker."

An argument that ended up with one party dead was never good. Did Sheriff Haak know? And if so, why didn't he mention the fight to Everly?

There was also the very real possibility that Haak hadn't bothered to ask too many questions. Maybe he knew nothing about Larry Walker.

Doubt snuck up on Wyatt. Was Haak simply old and tired of doing his job? Had he been sheriff so long that he didn't care? Or was it worse? Could the sheriff somehow be involved in Axl Baker's death— and the others in Las Vegas, besides?

True, Carl Haak didn't fit the typical age range of a serial killer. Most of killers hunted in their midtwenties to early thirties. But, he was a white male— the hallmark gender and race for most, if not all, serial killers.

It was an interesting theory that deserved to be explored more. Until then, it was up to Wyatt to find out all he could about Axl's last day in Pleasant Pines.

"Do you know what they argued about?" he asked.

The desk clerk shook her head. "Johanna didn't overhear much beyond raised voices and something about immigration."

"Could it have been migration? As in a wolf-pack migration?" Everly asked.

To Wyatt, the question made complete sense. Especially since Axl had come to the area to find a wolf pack migrating.

The desk clerk shrugged. "To be honest, I have no idea. I'm just telling you what Johanna told me. Like I said earlier, Everly, Johanna should be in by four o'clock."

"What about Larry?" asked Wyatt.

Darcy shook her head. "He's not on the schedule. I checked."

"Thanks, Darcy," said Everly.

Wyatt echoed, "Thanks."

"You're welcome, Wyatt," she called after them.

Without comment, Wyatt and Everly walked down the long corridor and stopped at the elevator as they waited for the doors to open. "How well do you know Darcy?" Everly asked.

He shrugged. "I don't know her, not really."

"She seems to know you."

Was Everly jealous? At least she was interested in his life. It had been years since anyone cared and Wyatt wasn't sure how he felt about the intrusion. The elevator doors opened, and he waited for Everly to enter.

"Small town, I guess," he said, following Everly. "Anyone new would cause a stir."

The doors closed and then they were alone. The exotically spicy scent of her perfume filled the tiny space, coating his skin and lingering on his lips. It was an exquisite torture to be alone with Everly and Wyatt's mind was occupied with images that were as sexy as her fragrance. His body reacted, reminding him how long he truly had been without a woman's touch.

"What do you think about what Darcy said?" Everly asked, interrupting Wyatt's thoughts. "Isn't it suspicious that my brother has an argument the night that he also happens to be murdered?"

"It's more than a little suspicious. It's something that Sheriff Haak should've known and investigated."

The elevator doors slid open and they stepped into the hall.

"My room's up here," said Everly. "Two twenty-three." She used a keycard to open the door and crossed the threshold.

From where he stood, Wyatt could clearly see two beds. His mind immediately returned to his sexy musings. From the hallway, he mumbled, "I'll wait here."

She seemed not to notice his reluctance and said, "It'll be one second."

For years, Wyatt had lived with the fact that he'd failed to catch a killer. It was a scab that he picked at every day, never allowing it to heal. Was he really willing to try and catch the serial killer again? And what if all ended badly a second time?

Maybe it was better if he stepped away from the investigation—and Everly—right now.

True, he'd promised to help her. Yet, weren't promises made to be broken?

Underneath it all, there was a magnetic pull toward the case. To ignore that draw went against everything Wyatt was—or at least, everything he used to be.

In less than a minute, Everly wheeled her suitcase from the room. Strapped to the handle was a laptop bag. "Let me get that for you," he said, reaching for the bag.

Everly released her grip on the handle. "Thanks." They walked back down the hallway and she pushed the button for the elevator. The doors opened immediately, and they were once again in the confines of the car. The air was heavy and settled on his flesh.

"What should we do about Larry Walker?" Everly asked as the elevator came to rest on the ground floor.

"Without question we need to look into the cook and the possibility that the argument became deadly."

"How do we do that? I've watched all sorts of cop shows over the years. Do we interrogate him?" she asked as they exited the elevator.

He laughed. "It's not quite that simple, even if you are a sworn law-enforcement officer. But, neither one of us has a badge, so we're on our own and can only learn what people are willing to share. I say we start by talking with the bartender."

"Darcy said that Johanna's shift starts at four." She removed the phone from her purse and brought up the home screen. "Which is now."

At the far side of the lobby stood the in-house

bar. Despite a sign that read, Open 5:00 p.m., the lights were on.

"Looks like she's right on time," said Wyatt.

With Everly's suitcase in tow, they entered the pub. A long mahogany bar filled one wall, shelves full of liquor bottles and several beer taps sat behind. A row of bar stools stood in front and more than a dozen tables filled the rest of the room. A TV hung on the wall. There was a cable news show on, but the sound was muted. A young woman with dark hair pulled into a ponytail stood next to a cash register. She looked up as Wyatt and Everly approached.

"Sorry, folks, we don't open until five o'clock. If you come back in an hour, I can get you a drink then."

"Are you Johanna?" Everly asked.

"I am."

"Mind if we ask you a few questions?" asked Wyatt. "It's about a customer who came in two nights ago. His name was Axl Baker."

Johanna's eyes widened with sudden recognition. "That means you must be Mr. Baker's sister. Darcy told me that you might stop by."

Despite the tears that shone in Everly's eyes, she nodded.

Wyatt saw the sadness in Everly's expression, and wondered what he should do. Take her hand? Squeeze her shoulder? Nothing seemed right, and it only made him want to get the answers she sought. He said, "So, you remember Axl Baker?"

"Of course, I remember him. He was really cute,

kind of hard to forget. Then the next day we all heard what happened. It was just real sad."

"We were told that you overheard an argument between the deceased and the hotel's cook. Do you know what they disagreed about?"

"It was pretty busy that night. But their voices were raised, and I heard a little bit of a quarrel over the other customers' conversations."

"What makes you say it was an argument?" asked Wyatt. He knew enough not to prejudge what had happened without more evidence. "If it was noisy, they might have been talking loud to be heard."

"It was their body language, too," said the bartender. "Larry poked Mr. Baker in the chest and Mr. Baker swiped away his hand."

"What happened next?" asked Everly.

"Then Larry sort of threw up his hands and I told him he couldn't argue with the customers and to go home. He left without causing a scene. Afterward I kind of made a joke that Mr. Baker shouldn't order anything from the menu, you know—because Larry's the cook and all."

"What did Mr. Baker do afterward?"

"He kind of laughed it off, then paid his bill and left."

Everly asked, "Do you remember what he had to drink?"

"Oddly enough, I do. It was a seltzer water and he left a tip that was twice the price of his drink."

Wyatt pictured the room as it would have been, filled with midweek customers. The two men, their discussion becoming heated. Words exchanged. One person had laid hands on the other. But did it end there? Did Larry go home and fume, getting angrier and angrier until he had to exact revenge? And while the scenario might fit a hundred other crimes, how did a serial killer play into the circumstances?

"Today's Larry's day off," said Johanna. "But I can text and let him know you're looking for him."

That was the last thing Wyatt wanted. "No thanks." He paused. "I do have one other question. Is Larry a native of Pleasant Pines?"

Johanna narrowed her eyes and pursed her lips. "I'm not sure where he's from originally. I've only been in town for a little over six years, but I do know he moved here from Las Vegas not much more than two and a half years ago."

Las Vegas? Everly felt herself shaking. There was a hot breath as Wyatt's whisper touched her neck. "Don't react here. Just listen to my voice and let's get to the truck."

Dazed, she let him maneuver her through the lobby. With a hip, he pushed open the door. Cold air and blowing snow hit Everly full in the face, shaking her from her state of shock. Drawing in a deep breath, she said, "I'm fine now."

Wyatt continued to hold her arm. She liked the feel of his strong hand on her flesh. The warmth of his body. The feel of his hot breath on her cool skin.

"Really?" he asked.

She feared that if he let go, she truly would fall.

But she'd die before admitting it. "I'm better, at least."

He opened the door to his truck and held Everly's hand as she climbed into the seat. He stowed her suitcase behind the bench and closed the door, then rounded to the driver's side. Everly concentrated on taking deep, cleansing breaths. She tried to clear her mind, just for a moment. Still, the fact that Larry Walker had moved from Las Vegas couldn't be ignored.

"Are you sure you're okay? You might be in shock, and getting hit in the head won't help anything," Wyatt said. "Maybe we should take you to see Doc Lambert."

"I'm fine," she said again. This time it was closer to the truth. "Las Vegas. That's something that links your old case to Larry Walker. The timing seemed right, too. It can't just be a coincidence."

Wyatt silently put the truck into Reverse and pulled out of the parking lot. He drove, his eyes on the road.

"I'd say Larry Walker is a decent suspect. He's better than the guy we arrested when I was with the Bureau."

"What do *we* do next?" she asked.

"We go back to my place and see what can be found about Larry Walker, formerly of Las Vegas. We check to see if he's got a criminal record. Employment history. Friends and family."

Everly sat back in the seat and stared out the window. The sky was a leaden gray and snow zoomed past like a million tiny stars. Had she really only been in Pleasant Pines for a few hours? It seemed like days. And yet, Wyatt Thornton was giving her the first shred of hope she'd had since she arrived. "I'm not sure that I've thanked you properly," she said.

"I'm not the kind of guy you should count on," he said. "I can run an internet search and ask a few questions."

"Not to be too forward," she said. "But you don't give yourself enough credit."

"Too forward?" he echoed with a laugh. "Everly, you have been nothing but forward since you tripped over me this morning."

She gave a quiet laugh. "Fair enough," she said. "I'm glad you knocked me over. You're a great resource—and someone I can trust."

"That's where you're wrong. You shouldn't trust me. I'm nobody's hero."

Everly glanced at Wyatt before looking back out the window. She wasn't some foolish girl, trying to find a man who needed fixing. If a guy came with a warning, she always listened.

Everly reminded herself, once again, that she didn't need the burden of romance. Especially if she wanted to figure out what happened to her brother.

Wyatt turned on to the long drive and his house came into view. It stood on a rise, with a thick copse of trees nearby. To her, it looked as if the home part of the landscape, like the Rocky Mountains, the forest, or the sky.

"This house must have a lot of history," she said. "How'd you come to own a place like this?"

"I was given a really good severance package when I left the FBI. It paid for the house and gave me enough to live on for a couple of years."

That answered some of Everly's questions, but not all of them. "Why Wyoming? How'd you pick Pleasant Pines and this house in particular?"

"I was angry when I left the Bureau," he said. The truck slowed as they neared the house and Wyatt parked next to Everly's rental car. "At first, I wanted to get away from everything and everyone. No connections. Nothing. One day, I stumbled on Pleasant Pines and stopped at the diner on Main Street."

"The one you took me to earlier?" she asked, then rolled her eyes. "Please don't tell me you decided to stay because of the apple pie."

He turned off the engine but stayed in his seat. "To be honest, I don't know why I stayed. But I found a Realtor and she brought me here. Nobody had lived in this house for years—a decade almost. You should have seen it then. Peeling paint. Rotted roof. Crumbling porch."

Everly could well imagine the house and Wyatt's labor of love.

He continued, "Because it was in such rough shape, I got a great deal. I adopted Gus from a local shelter. The house needed a lot of work and those renovations occupied my time. Made it harder for me to think about…things I didn't want to think about. There's not much else to tell."

He opened his door and stepped from the truck, and Everly assumed he was done talking. Following suit, Everly hopped down just as Wyatt rounded to the passenger side. He hefted her suitcase from behind the seat and carried her bag to the door.

"I haven't had a guest before, but we can make do," Wyatt said. "The sofa's comfortable enough."

No guests? No job? No more repairs? "What is it that you do out here?"

"I walk my dog."

"That's a lot of walking."

"I go into town once a week for supplies. I stop in at Sally's and get pie and coffee. What else do I need?"

"It sounds about as opposite to my life as you can get. I work for a public relations firm in downtown Chicago and my schedule is nothing but meetings, lunches and dinner parties. And you know what? I love my job. I wouldn't have it any other way."

Wyatt kicked open the door and slapped a switch, turning on an overhead light. "After what happened to me in Vegas, I'd never go back to living at lightning speed."

His words came out with venom. Her face burned. Obviously, she'd said something wrong. "I never meant to suggest that you should. Or to criticize your life here," she began. He stared at her, his eyes as dark and stormy as the sky. Everly's words failed her. "It's just that we're different, that's all."

Wyatt cleared his throat. "I guess we are."

For the first time, Everly understood that she'd

been hoping that somehow, she and Wyatt Thornton were compatible—the wish was so secret that she hadn't even acknowledged it herself—and only felt disappointment once it was gone.

Gus ambled into the room and greeted them with a happy bark and a madly wagging tail.

Cold from the outside had crept into the house and the room held a chill. Wyatt knelt at the hearth and within minutes, flames crackled in the fireplace, filling the room with light and warmth. She sank into the sofa. Tension that she hadn't realized she'd been holding slipped from her neck.

Padding softly across the floor, Gus approached and put his head in Everly's lap. She stroked his ears and the dog closed his eyes, sighing in complete bliss. "If only it were that easy," Everly said.

"Pardon?" Wyatt stood. His body was backlit by the flames and Everly swallowed. He was strong, solid and unyielding—much like the mountains around his home.

Looking back at the dog, Everly said, "If only it were so easy to be at peace. Just a warm lap and someone to scratch you behind the ears."

"It's a whole lot easier to be tranquil when you only focus on what's important." He stoked the logs with a poker. "It's why I left the FBI."

"Have you found it, yet?" she asked. "Peace?"

Wyatt sniffed and Everly lifted her gaze. "Not exactly, but I'm closer than I was." He turned to a desk that sat in the corner and opened a drawer. After pulling out three accordion files, he returned to Everly's side. He let them drop and they hit the sofa with a *thwack*.

"What's all this?" Everly asked.

Wyatt sat down on the opposite side of the pile. "This," he said handing the top file to Everly, "is everything I saved from my final case in Vegas. Some of it is just media reports. Some are my notes. Some is confidential—but nobody asked for anything back when I left, and I sorta kept it all. I also have a flash drive with information on each of the victims' social media accounts and some pictures we took at the time of the murders. I also have copies of every victim's text messages and emails."

"Let's start with all of your hard copies." Peeling back the flap, Everly removed several sheets of paper.

"It's all in chronological order," he said.

Everly read through several police reports and couldn't help but wonder how often Wyatt looked through these files. Had he spent years perusing these same pages as he searched for clues that he'd missed?

She'd never ask, but somehow knew that her suspicion was right.

Everly held a newspaper article, probably one of the final ones written.

It was much like what she'd found on the internet earlier in the day. Over the course of eighteen months, five men had been murdered. It wasn't until corpse number three turned up that the local police involved the FBI.

At the time the article was published, a blackjack dealer was in custody and prime suspect. Yet, Everly knew that eventually, he'd been set free.

"You arrested one man for the crimes," said Everly. "What made him a suspect?"

"Serial killers seek to relive their crimes. They take trophies from the victims. They can also leave calling cards. It was my belief then, as it is now, that the killer keeps the other halves of the two-dollar bills found with the bodies. Another way that the killers relive their kill is to revisit the scene. The blackjack dealer made trips to all the sites where bodies were found. He attended all press conferences and discussed the murders in general with his coworkers. He fit the profile," said Wyatt. "So, we brought him in."

"Aside from Larry is there anyone local you suspect?"

"Until a few hours ago, I didn't have any reason to suspect anyone of any crimes. Give me a bit to see what I can find."

"We," Everly corrected. "What we can find."

"We," said Wyatt with a snort.

The conversation waned and Everly turned her attention back to the stack of papers she held. The next sheet was a letter from the Office of Professional Responsibility for the Federal Bureau of Investigation.

The letter stated that the OPR had opened an investigation into the conduct of Wyatt R. Thornton for suppressing an alibi that cleared the dealer from one of the murders—and therefore exonerating him from all of the crimes.

Due to the egregious violation of Bureau policy, the OPR recommended that Wyatt's position be terminated.

A handwritten note was scrawled across the bottom of the page. It stated simply that, "Thornton has chosen to resign. No further action will be taken."

Everly felt ill and slipped the letter back into the file folder. Had Wyatt's lie ruined his career? Was he really so bent on appearing to solve the case that he was willing to let an innocent man go to jail?

If he was, what did that mean for Everly—and her search for Axl's killer?

Chapter 5

Wyatt's eyes burned. He'd looked at all these documents hundreds of times. Hell, maybe even thousands. There was nothing new to see, and yet, he had sat and shuffled through papers as the snow quietly fell and covered the ground.

He flipped over a piece of paper and set it in the appropriate stack. There were still thousands of documents remaining. "I've looked at all of this before," he said. "Every damned time I go through the file, I think I'll find something that I missed before."

"What about now?" Everly asked as she rolled her shoulders. Reaching her arms above her head, she arched her back.

The thin material of her sweater strained against her breasts and the hollow of her neck was visible.

For a moment, he imagined what it would feel like to slide his lips over the spot, to kiss his way lower, until— "Sorry, what did you say?" *Busted.*

"What about now?" she asked.

What about now, indeed?

"Did you find anything new?"

He shook his head. "Nothing."

"What should we do next?" she asked.

"Let's take a break and eat something. Then we'll get back to reading these documents to see if there's something—anything—that has been overlooked. I've got a pizza in the freezer. It's not fancy but it is edible."

"Edible is my favorite kind of food," Everly joked.

Getting to his feet, Wyatt took the pizza from the freezer to thaw a bit on the counter while he let the oven preheat. "It'll be ready in a bit," he said.

"Isn't there more we can do—about the case, I mean?"

"Unfortunately, most cases are like a puzzle—but we're looking for the piece that doesn't quite fit." He stood. Blood flooded his legs in a hot rush and his feet tingled with pins and needles. It had been too long since he'd studied a case for hours. The aches and pains were minor when compared to the gale of adrenaline that blew threw him.

"Sounds tedious," Everly said in response to his previous comment.

"More than tedious, it can be downright mundane. Until it's not." Wyatt slid the pizza onto a baking sheet, then put it into the oven.

"When does that happen?"

"When you find something important. That's the worst of it," he said. "With an investigation, you can't make something happen—as tempting as it sometimes seems."

"Why did you choose to focus on investigating serial killers anyway?" she asked. "What was the draw?"

Wyatt hadn't meant to start a conversation about his past life. He knew that he could stop it with a brusque reply. Yet, he drew in a lungful of air and exhaled slowly. "Tracking a killer is usually about trying to understand how the killer thinks and predict their next move. Solving a puzzle. Looking for that missing piece is mundane, like I said—but it can also drag you into the darkness."

Even in the firelight, Wyatt could see Everly's cheeks redden. "It sounds like more than a job, but it was a calling."

She was right. But there was so much more to it—the camaraderie of the team, their dependence on each other. Knowing too well that their backup was often the only thing that gave him clarity as he lost himself in the depths of an investigation.

Not for the first time, Wyatt felt a connection to Everly. First it had been physical, now it was emotional. God, he wanted to kiss her, make that connection complete. Then he would finally know if her lips were as soft and full as they looked.

Wyatt forced his libido to chill and moved to the window. Wind buffeted the house as drifts of white snow blew past. He needed to concentrate. He hadn't caught the serial killer in Vegas and he'd had the full support of the FBI behind him. Back then, he didn't have any distractions like Everly Baker, either.

For the first time in years, Wyatt was having company for dinner. Or any meal really. He'd come to Wyoming for seclusion and to turn his back on all of society. But as Everly moved to the kitchen table, making stacks out of his clutter, Wyatt felt a warming in his chest. It was tempting to think that somehow his life had changed with Everly's arrival. But he was smarter than that and this moment of domesticity was fleeting and fragile as a single snowflake.

Wyatt knew if he wanted to find this killer, he needed a focus. One that was so narrow it didn't have room for romance.

Everly stood at the sink and rinsed the final plate.

"You don't have to do that," Wyatt said for what felt like the hundredth time. "I can do my own dishes."

Everly tucked the plate into the dishwasher and dried her hands on a towel. "I was brought up to be a good houseguest," she said, joking slightly. "If someone makes me a delicious dinner, I can at least clean up afterward."

"It was just a frozen pizza," he said.

She threaded the towel through the refrigerator's handle. "It wasn't freshly made, deep-dish-pizza good, but it was tasty." She turned to Wyatt and winked, to show that she was still teasing.

He gave a snort of a laugh.

"Next time I'll let you make me dinner," he said. "Maybe some famous Chicago-style pizza."

Her chest constricted, squeezing her heart. "Will there be a next time? Don't you think that Sheriff Haak is going to kick me out of town? I've definitely become persona non grata."

"You aren't going anywhere until we figure out what happened to your brother. In fact…" He paused and pivoted to face the desk. "Let's do a little internet snooping and see what we can find out about Larry Walker—the cook from the Pleasant Pines Inn who argued with your brother."

Wyatt pulled a kitchen chair up next to his desk for Everly and then sat in his own seat. He powered up the computer and entered a few keystrokes. "I paid a fee for access to a site that finds criminal records."

She scooted closer and examined the screen. A previous search bar was open and filled with three words. Axl James Baker. Her throat felt raw, like she had just swallowed a handful of gravel. When she spoke, the words were filled with flint. "You looked up my brother? Why would you do that?"

He glanced her way and then looked back at the screen. "Your brother's corpse was found on my property. You think I wouldn't be curious?"

Everly admitted he had point, even if she wasn't willing to say so out loud. "I thought you said you didn't want to be involved."

"I might not want to actively investigate a suspicious death—to take responsibility for clearing up a mystery. Tell me who wouldn't want to know more about a dead person found on their property?" He exhaled and turned away. "I didn't mean to upset you by digging into your brother's background. But I'm not going to apologize for looking. Especially since it's the only way to help gather information that might lead us to our suspect." After clearing Axl's name, Wyatt began to type.

She wanted to pursue the conversation, but how? Wyatt Thornton was proving to be an enigma and yet she sensed one thing. Wyatt was more than alone—he was also lonely. She returned her attention to the computer screen.

On a different website, Wyatt spent a few minutes finding Larry Walker's birth date. Then, Larry Walker's details, along with the locations of Las Vegas, Nevada and Pleasant Pines, Wyoming, had been entered into the original search field.

One hundred and twenty-eight hits were found.

Everly pointed at the number. "Seems like Larry has been busy being bad."

"It does," said Wyatt. He clicked on the first link. "Assault. Pleasant Pines, Wyoming. Seven months ago. Looks like Larry got into a bar fight at the Pleasant Pines Inn. He spent the night in jail and was fined five hundred dollars and released."

Wyatt scrolled through the list. "Assault. Larceny. Driving under the influence. Possession of a controlled substance."

"Doesn't sound like a nice guy. In fact, his criminal record makes him look like a total creep."

"It does," said Wyatt. He leaned back in his chair and cradled his head in his hands. "And that is what bothers me. Most serial killers aren't crooks and delinquents. They're methodical. They fit in to society, so nobody suspects them of anything—especially nothing so horrible as murder. They're violent, sure, but it's like the cold precision of a scalpel. This guy is an inferno—out of control and raging hot."

"The way I see it is that this Larry guy is violent and that's all that counts."

"That's just it—I'm not saying that Larry wouldn't hurt someone. He will. He has. In fact, I think he could actually kill someone."

"There you have it," said Everly. "He's capable of murder."

Wyatt held up a hand. "Not so fast. Larry would beat a person to death. Or shoot them in a fury. Not pump alcohol into their system and then leave them outside to freeze to death."

"Is that what you think happened to my brother?"

Wyatt sighed. "I do. There's no other explanation."

"But why?"

"*Why* was the one question I could never figure out. I guess that's how I never caught the guy. As far as the FBI is concerned, there are four things that define a serial killer. First is that the same kind of attack is repeated over time."

"As in a series of murders," said Everly. "Hence, a serial killer."

"Exactly," said Wyatt. "The second is that the methodology is the same. They might get more efficient, but the mode of killing never varies."

"So, all of these men were given too much alcohol and, once incapacitated, left for dead."

"That's how we know all the deaths are connected, and it was unquestionable once the link was made with half of a two-dollar bill found in their wallet."

"Did you ever try to get fingerprints from the money?"

"During the investigation, we got fingerprints from everything. Nothing turned up on the money—aside from thousands of other partial prints—and no two were the same. We figured our doer wore gloves. Still, we can ask the sheriff to run prints on the bill found in your brother's wallet."

Just thinking about the stubborn cop left Everly frustrated. "Do you think he'll do that for us?"

Wyatt sighed. "I have no idea."

"What about finding other fingerprints? The killer couldn't have worn gloves all the time. They had to have made a mistake once."

"The problem with the killer in Vegas, and here, is that the deaths all looked natural. After the victim's been buried—or worse, cremated—there's very little or no evidence to be collected."

"Too bad it hadn't been that easy." She hated to hear about the perverse mind of a serial killer, but if she was going to find justice for Axl, she needed to understand everything. "What else do serial killers have in common? You said there were four hallmarks."

"Third is that the victims are similar. Same gender. Same build. Same race. Same hair and eye color. In other words, they have a preference in the type of victims and the killings aren't random."

Everly stomach roiled. "It's all too twisted."

Wyatt nodded. "Then the last factor isn't going to make you feel any better."

"Which is?"

"There's usually a sexual nature to the crime. And that's one thing in this case that had me stumped. There was no sign of sexual contact between the victims and the killer—consensual or otherwise."

"Then why do you assume there was a sexual element?"

"It could have been one-sided. Perhaps the killer masturbated into a condom at the scene. Or maybe he took pictures and used them for gratification later. Or maybe there was another motive entirely."

"If everything you said is true, and the serial killer is active in Wyoming, then there have to be more victims here."

Wyatt leaned forward and brought up another website.

"The *Pleasant Pines Gazette*," she said, reading the masthead.

"The sheriff mentioned that he sees deaths like your brother's all the time."

"He did," said Everly. "He even brought up the fact that Axl might've had too much to drink and that's how he got lost. Funny that it turned out just like he predicted." Everly shivered. "Do you think he's involved?"

"Sheriff Haak?" Wyatt shook his head. "No way."

Everly wasn't willing to let go of her theory so easily. "Isn't Haak the one investigating all the killings? Who better to be the killer than the man who determined the deaths to be accidental?"

"For one thing," said Wyatt. "He doesn't have a connection to Las Vegas. You heard him. He's lived in Pleasant Pines his entire life."

"He could have traveled back and forth between Wyoming and Nevada," she said, realizing even as she said it that Wyatt was right. Haak wasn't guilty of anything beyond overlooking some pretty subtle clues.

Wyatt spoke. "What I do think is that this has happened before enough times that Haak recognizes the situation. Yet it hasn't happened so much that he's gotten suspicious. He's not wrong, Everly, when he says that people die of exposure out here all the time. Which is why it could be especially tough to catch whoever did this."

Wyatt navigated the newspaper's site, pulling up the police blotter. He entered several phrases. *Death from exposure. Blood-alcohol content. Male.*

"Try searching 'out of town,' too," suggested Everly.

Wyatt did as she advised and then hit the magnifying glass icon. The search lasted only a few seconds and a list of five men appeared. The first death had happened a little less than three years ago. The last was from the day before yesterday. Axl James Baker. Wyatt hit the print icon and a sleeping printer sprang to life and whirred as it reproduced the police reports for each of the men.

Wyatt retrieved the sheets and stood reading by the firelight. Everly approached and peered over his shoulder. "The circumstances are all the same," said Everly. "I can't believe that nobody put all of this evidence together until now."

"Pleasant Pines doesn't have a large police force and the technology they use is pretty dated. All the killings are months apart and each one has a natural cause of death."

"Are you saying that they aren't connected?"

"No, I think they're probably connected, all right. It's just that I can see how the sheriff missed all the links."

"Look at this." She pointed to one page. "They all stayed at the Pleasant Pines Inn. It's where Larry works." Excitement coursed through Everly's veins. "In the morning, we can take this information to the sheriff and force him to open an investigation."

Wyatt shook his head.

"Why not?"

"We need something more substantial than five bodies who happened to stay at the only hotel in town. Until we have concrete evidence that connects the cases *and* a solid suspect, I don't want to make accusations," Wyatt said.

Everly knew that past accusations had cost Wyatt his job. He was obviously reluctant to make the same mistake. Yet, without Wyatt she'd have a hard time convincing the sheriff to even consider that Axl had been murdered.

"What more do you need besides all these deaths and Larry's connection to Las Vegas?" Everly asked.

"I want to see if any of the other victims were found with half of a two-dollar bill."

"And do you have a website that can tell you that?"

"I don't."

Wyatt turned to her. Firelight danced on his face, his shoulders, his torso. An inner fire sprang to life in her middle, consuming her until she was nothing but ash blowing in the storm. She looked away.

"What do we do now?" How many times had she asked that same question of Wyatt? And yet, he always had an answer.

"We need to look at the list of personal belongings for all the men. Sheriff Haak has those in his files, I'm sure. I'm just as certain that he won't share them with us." He paused and slipped a hand into his back pocket. He withdrew a slip of paper and held it up to the light. "I think I know what we can do, though."

Everly looked at the phone number. Underneath it was three words: Rocky Mountain Justice.

Snow swirled, rising and falling on currents of air. The night was vast and endless—an ocean of darkness. And then the Darkness took form. Snow crunched underfoot. The cold, biting and burning, was nothing compared to the heat of hatred that filled the Darkness to the very core.

"'And when he had opened the fourth seal, I heard the voice of the fourth beast say, "Come and see." And I looked, and behold, a pale horse.'" The words hovered, a mist in the cold, only to be swept away by the wind.

The old farmhouse sat alone. The windows were ablaze with light and the scene within was visible, even at a distance. The two of them stood next to the table, shoulders close but not touching.

The woman's hair fell forward, and she tucked a lock behind her ear. Wyatt watched her, as if he could drink in the woman and her gesture. The woman didn't interest the Darkness. She wasn't its to claim. And yet, here she was—with Wyatt.

Dense and heavy loathing filled the Darkness until it could crush the world.

Continuing, the Darkness said, "'And his name that sat on him was Death, and Hell followed with him.'"

In the distance, Wyatt lifted his head and looked to the window. Had he heard the words? Did he see the Darkness? Sense its presence?

Sometimes the Darkness thought Wyatt knew and was still playing the game. But he never made a move, not even when the bodies began to turn up in Wyoming. It was if he had forgotten who he was and what he needed to do. They were the opposite sides of the same coin, Wyatt and the Darkness. That's why the latest body had to be brought to his property. It was a trap to draw in Wyatt. And draw him in it had.

But the woman was in Wyatt's home. At his table. Smiling at him, as if she understood. She wasn't part of the game and her presence could ruin everything.

Well, that wasn't going to happen. And sadly, there was no helping her now. She had to be devoured by the Darkness.

Wyatt folded the pillow over and adjusted it under his neck. He flipped to his back and stared at the ceiling. Even though it was the middle of the night, moonlight seeped in around the curtain's edge. He'd been asleep, yet something had awakened him. What? He didn't know. The air crackled with static, as if lightning had struck in the room.

On the floor, in his dog bed, Gus growled in his sleep.

Rolling to his side, Wyatt spied the dog. Head up, ears alert, Gus looked at the door.

"What is it, boy?" he whispered.

Another growl, this one deeper.

Wyatt sat up. The covers slid down his torso and pooled in his lap. He strained to hear. The silence was complete, not even interrupted by the occasional creak of the settling foundation or the wind in the eaves. It was as if the house was holding its breath.

He exhaled.

Wyatt reached for the bedside light. His fingers

brushed the cold metal at the lamp's base. He hesitated, not bothering with the switch. Blindly, he opened the drawer of the bedside table instead. Hidden in the back, behind a book, was a SIG Sauer. It was empty, but a full magazine was tucked in next to the gun.

He shoved the clip home and pulled back on the slide, chambering a round.

Wyatt set his feet on the floor and stood. The old boards creaked in protest.

"Gus," he said in a harsh whisper. "Stay."

Treading lightly, he moved to the door and into the corridor. A small, circular window at the end of the hallway let in silvery light. Wyatt glanced outside. The storm had stopped, and a full moon hung in the sky. He peered down at the snow-covered ground. There, clear in the lunar glow, was a set of footprints.

He froze. Blinked. Looked again.

No doubt there was a single set of footprints leading to his back door. None going away. But he'd locked the back door. Hadn't he? He tried to recall those awkward moments as he'd left Everly and checked all the points of entry while she settled on the sofa and couldn't remember if he had.

Had he really been so careless, tonight of all nights?

Without question, someone had come to his home. Were they inside right now? If they were—well, then it was a game of cat and mouse.

Rushing to the stairs, Wyatt pressed his back into the wall and glanced into the yawning abyss of the stairwell. Moving as quietly as possible, he descended to the landing. From there, he glanced down again. The entire living room was visible from where he hid.

The fire was low in the grate. Cold seeped up the stairs, icy tendrils snaking around his bare feet and ankles.

Everly stood in the middle of the living room. The unmistakable glint of a metal blade was at her neck. The perpetrator was hidden behind her, face obscured. His heart raced. His palms grew damp and a bead of sweat trickled down his back.

The knife flashed, nicking Everly's skin. Like a seam had opened, a bead of red blood gathered on her throat. She shrieked. A shadow took form and rushed from the room. The back door shut with a crack.

Wyatt sprinted through the living room and pushed against the door. It didn't budge. He fumbled with the doorknob and leaned his shoulder into the door, knowing it was a smart move on the intruder's part. Barricade the door. Wyatt was trapped—a prisoner in his own home.

He kicked the wood. The door gave. Gun drawn and at the ready, Wyatt ran into the night. His bare feet sank in fresh snow. The cold left his bones brittle and seared his flesh. He ignored the discomfort and pressed on. But to go where? A gust of wind blew, erasing the footprints and leaving Wyatt alone in the darkness.

Chapter 6

In the distance, taillights appeared near the end of his drive as a car sped away. Wyatt leveled his gun at the retreating auto, took aim and pulled the trigger twice. He felt the recoil in his shoulder. The boom expanded to the edges of the horizon, as the stench of cordite was swept away by the wind. The car fishtailed as it rocketed away, disappearing into the night.

Wyatt cursed and returned to the house. He examined the door on the way in. Scratches had been gouged into the wood, where the door had been pried open. He slammed the door shut.

Every light on the ground floor was illuminated and Everly stood inside the threshold. A wound on her neck trickled blood. "I heard gunshots. Did you get him?"

His galloping pulse slowed as he shook his head. "I don't think I hit anything." Then he asked, "How are you? You're cut. Is anything else hurt?"

She touched the wound. Her fingers trembled. "I think I'm okay. This is just a little scratch. I should get cleaned up, though."

He recalled the metal blade pressed into her flesh and went cold with dread for what might've been. He pulled out a kitchen chair. "Sit," he said. "Let me help you."

Everly dropped to the seat. Wyatt set his firearm aside and wet a kitchen towel before dabbing at the cut on Everly's throat. The slash was short, only two inches long, and thankfully shallow. The bleeding was already slowing. "I don't think you'll need stitches," he said. "But you might end up with a little bit of a scar."

"Who cares about a scar?" she asked, her voice cracked. "What just happened?"

It was exactly what Wyatt wanted to know. As far as he knew, she was the only person to meet this killer twice and survive. "What do you remember?"

"I was asleep," she said, "and I woke up with a knife at my throat." She shut her eyes as a shudder wracked her body and tears threatened to leak from her eyes.

Wyatt waited while she gave in to the terror she'd been holding back. She needed only a moment to let it out and pull herself back together.

Everly swallowed and wiped her eyes with the back of her hand. Taking a deep breath to steady herself, she continued her story. "I was pulled to my feet. I was so frightened I couldn't even speak. I heard Gus upstairs. He was growling, and then..."

"I showed up a moment later," Wyatt offered.

"Yeah," she said with a nod.

Wyatt pulled open a couple of drawers, shuffling around until he found a tube of antiseptic ointment, gauze and medical tape. He tended to her neck without speaking. Wyatt thought of a million questions he wanted answered and yet, there was only one that really mattered. "Why are you alive?"

"Excuse me?"

Wyatt had lived alone for more than three years. Yet he hadn't been on his own long enough to mistake the tone of Everly's question as anything other than being insulted.

Yet this wasn't the time to worry about being polite. If he was going to catch this killer once and for all, he had to understand everything.

"Why didn't the killer cut your neck while you slept? Or why weren't you smothered after you'd been knocked unconscious at the hotel? Why are you still alive?"

Everly pressed the heels of her hands into her eye sockets. "I've asked myself that same question again and again."

"Do you have an answer?" There was one thing that Wyatt was certain of now. The killer's reluctance to murder Everly was the key to discovering his identity.

She exhaled and let her arms drop to her sides. "No," she said. "Not really."

God, she was beautiful. He wanted to take her into his arms and offer her comfort and solace. He wanted more. "You look tired," he said instead. "Why don't you go up to my room and get some rest?"

She shook her head. "There's no way I can sleep now."

"You might be surprised." Wyatt stood in front of Everly and held out his hand.

Everly stared at his outstretched fingers for a moment before placing her hand in his. It was there again. The warmth. The tingle. The connection. He pulled Everly to her feet and she stood slowly. "Thanks," she said.

"I'll even let you keep Gus in the room with you," Wyatt said, trying to lighten the mood, and at the same time knowing that Gus was a vigilant protector. "He'll keep you safe."

"And what will you do?" Everly asked.

"Me? I'll be fine down here."

Everly pressed her lips together, an argument ready to break free, no doubt.

Before she could argue or demur, Wyatt pointed to the stairs. "I insist."

"Thanks," Everly said, with a yawn. Even after everything that had happened to her, she'd be asleep within minutes. Or maybe she'd be asleep because of everything that had happened.

He watched as she walked to the stairs and disappeared past the landing. When he was alone, Wyatt moved to the front window and looked out at the night. He saw nothing but felt as if there were eyes everywhere.

"Come and get me, you bastard," he muttered. He aimed the gun at his own reflection in the glass. Sliding his finger onto the trigger, he continued, "This time, I'll be ready."

Everly sighed and rolled over. Her wound touched the pillow and she grimaced. She flipped to her back and the throbbing in her head began anew. "Wyoming sucks," she said out loud.

On the floor next to her, Gus whined.

"Sorry for waking you," she said to the dog.

Funny, but Gus was easier to talk to than most humans. He was definitely easier to converse with than his owner. Wyatt Thornton had built such an impenetrable wall around himself that Everly imagined she could see the concrete and rebar. Not that she blamed Wyatt and yet, she couldn't help but think he would be well-served to get out of the house more. Heck, maybe he should make a friend or two.

Then again, his problems weren't hers and she had plenty of troubles of her own. Rolling to the other side, she finally found a position without discomfort. Her eyelids felt heavy and sleep began to claim her...

An icy shard of pain stabbed her chest and Everly sat up, breathing hard. Had she heard something downstairs? She strained to listen, hearing only her racing heart and labored breathing.

There it was, a howl. The wind? A wolf? The

killer, returned? Everly reached for the bedside lamp and turned it on. The room blazed with light. She glanced at Gus. He was lying in his bed, blinking.

Sure, the dog seemed nonplussed, yet Everly knew that she had heard something...

Moreover, there was no way that Everly was going to lie in bed and allow herself to be attacked a second time.

Wyatt stretched out as much as the sofa would allow. His feet dangled over the edge and he figured that this was as comfortable as he could get. A creaking came from upstairs. Wyatt sat up, reaching for the gun.

It had to be Everly. Unless it wasn't.

She appeared on the landing. His fingers twitched with the need to touch her.

"I thought I heard something," she said. "It was like a howl."

Wyatt exhaled. "It's the wind in the eaves," he said. He set aside the gun. "I should've warned you. It can seem pretty loud upstairs, especially during a storm."

"Okay," she said, pivoting to go back up the stairs. "Thanks for letting me know. Good night."

Wyatt wasn't good at dealing with people, not anymore at least. And being helpful? Forget about it. All the same, he said, "I can check upstairs, make sure that it's only the wind. It might help you sleep better."

She gazed up the stairs, and Wyatt was certain she

was going to decline his offer. After a moment, she turned back to him. "Sure, that'd be nice."

She wore a pair of loose pajama pants in a blush rose. They hung low at her waist. A cream-colored tank top skimmed her body like a second skin. She ascended the stairs and Wyatt followed, mesmerized by the sway of her hips and the perfect form of her butt.

He forced his gaze to move and he looked over her shoulder, at once seeing Gus's smiling face at the top of the stairs.

"Hey, boy," he said, scratching the dog's head as he passed. "You keeping Everly safe for me?"

The second floor of Wyatt's home consisted of a master suite with its own bathroom. At one time, the suite had been two separate rooms and a closet. Before Wyatt moved in, he'd modernized the space. The rest of the second floor, not so much. There was a hall bath that had last been remodeled at the end of World War II and two small bedrooms filled with stuff that Wyatt no longer used but lacked the motivation to discard.

He pushed open the first door. Downhill skis. Cross-country skis. Snowshoes. A mountain bike with a broken chain and flat tire. "Everything looks in order," he said.

"Are you sure?" asked Everly. "I mean, how can you tell?"

"I can tell," Wyatt snapped. Who was she to question how he lived? True, he hadn't gone skiing the whole time he'd been living in Wyoming. And the mountain bike? It had sat, in need of repair, for over eighteen months.

Everly lifted her hands in surrender. "There's just a lot to keep track of, that's all."

"Chaos is the natural order," he said. "Did you know that?"

Everly shook her head. "I did not, and I didn't mean to offend you, either. I guess I shouldn't be speaking my mind so freely," she said.

"Apology accepted," said Wyatt. He moved to the second room and paused at the door. "This is where I kept all the notes from all the cases I've ever worked. It's a lot and I'm warning you now."

She inhaled and noisily exhaled. Shaking out arms and legs, she said, "I'm ready."

He was beginning to appreciate her frankness and her sense of humor, especially after the horror of earlier that night. He couldn't help but smile. "Smart-ass," he said, teasing.

Turning to the room, he flipped the light switch. It was just as he expected. Towering from floor to ceiling, dozens of boxes were stacked on top of each other. They ringed the wall and created a corridor through the middle of the room.

Everly came up behind him, so close he felt the heat from her body. The hairs on the back of his neck stood on end. "Wow," she said. "That is a lot of cases."

"I was the top behavioral scientist for the Bureau," he said. "I used to travel all over the world and consult on cases of all kinds."

"You should write a book," said Everly. "It'd be a blockbuster."

"The thought has crossed my mind before," he said. "But I put that part of my life behind me and I intend to leave it in the past," he said.

She didn't say anything, only nodded. It left Wyatt wondering her thoughts on the matter. Then again, why should he care? He continued, changing the subject completely, "Anyway, nothing's been moved in this room. It's exactly like I left it after coming up for the old case file this morning."

He turned to leave and came face-to-face with Everly. Her breasts pressed against his chest. The shadow of her nipples was unmistakable under the thin fabric of her tank top. He could see her pulse flutter at the base of her neck. His skin tingled, and his own heart began to race. "I'll just..." he began. His eyes were drawn to her lips and he forgot his next words. Pointing to the bathroom, he said, "I need to look in there."

"Oh, sure," she said.

He stepped to the side. She mirrored his movement. "Sorry, I'll go this way."

He stepped back. She did, too.

Wyatt placed his hands on her shoulders. God, she was so soft. A spicy sweetness still surrounded her like a halo. He looked at her mouth and licked his lips, hungry to kiss her. Yet, he knew that he had to remain professional. Not that being professional wasn't a good idea, it's just that Wyatt wasn't in the mood to make respectable decisions right now.

Hands still on her shoulders, Wyatt said, "You stay here."

He stepped past her and turned on the bathroom light. White and black tiles. Claw-foot tub. Shower curtain on a circular rod. Pedestal sink. It was just as it should be, down to the sliver of soap sitting in an indent on the back of the sink.

"There's no one else in this house," he said, "except you and me."

Gus whimpered from his place on the threshold.

"You, and me, and Gus," Wyatt amended.

She nodded. "Well, then." Hitching her chin toward the master bedroom, she continued, "I guess I better…"

"Sure," he said. He gestured to the stairs. "I should go."

"G'night, then."

Gus came to stand at Everly's side, and she stroked his ears. Gus sighed contentedly.

Lucky dog.

Wyatt felt the void in his own chest. Funny, he thought he'd gotten used to the solitude and now Wyatt wished that Everly would stay up a little more and talk. When had he last craved company? Turning, he moved to the stairs.

"Wyatt." She'd spoken his name softly, musically.

He froze with one of his feet hovering above the abyss.

"Wyatt," she said again.

This time he looked toward her.

"Do you mind?" she asked. Using her thumb, she

pointed to the bedroom. "I hate to be so forward, but…" She swallowed.

Wyatt's jaw tensed.

"Will you sleep with me?"

Everly could tell by Wyatt's widened eyes that he'd misunderstood her request. Then again, she'd been naive in the extreme not to realize the sexual implication. Her cheeks flamed red and hot. She cleared her throat and tried again.

"I've been attacked twice today. My brother was murdered. I don't know when I'll ever feel safe again, but I definitely won't be able to sleep by myself. I don't snore too much," she said, making light of the awkward moment.

Wyatt climbed the stairs that separated them and came to stand on the landing until he was only inches away from her. Heat radiated off his body, igniting something deep inside her.

"How do you know you can trust me?" he asked. His voice was dark as midnight and smooth as velvet.

For a moment, she was breathless with longing.

After realizing that she'd stood mute for a moment too long, she began speaking. "Well, obviously you aren't the person who gave me this." She touched the cut on her throat. "Which means you didn't give me this, either." Her fingers grazed the goose egg at the back of her skull. "Which means you aren't a threat and so…" She shrugged. "You're the one guy I can trust."

She raked her fingers through her hair and let out

all the air from her lungs. "Never mind. This has been a horrible day and I can see from the look on your face that I'm asking too much."

"I think wanting someone with you for protection and comfort makes sense, Everly."

"But I'm asking too much from *you*," she said.

"I'm not used to sharing anything," he said. "Especially, these days, my bed."

Her face felt as if it was on fire. Thank goodness the lights were off, and he couldn't see her blushing. "You'll be downstairs for protection, right? And I have Gus here for company." The dog ambled to Everly's side and leaned into her. She ran her fingers through the downy fur on the top of his head.

She waited a minute for Wyatt to say something. But what else needed to be said? With a nod of resignation, she stepped into the room.

"Everly," he said. His voice was smoke—dusky and dangerous. "Wait."

She paused but didn't turn around. The floorboard behind her creaked with his approach. Wyatt's breath warmed her shoulder.

"You're wrong," he whispered. "You can't trust me, and I don't think you need a man as shattered as I am right now." His fingertips brushed against her collarbone and his hand trailed from her shoulder to her arm. "And if you and I get in that bed, I promise you that sleeping is the last thing I'd want to do."

His whispered words washed over her. A shiver traveled through Everly. It wasn't from fear...but desire.

Holding her breath, Everly stood in the middle of

the room. She waited a minute…and a minute more. When she turned, he had gone. Padding softly across the floor, she slipped under the covers. She called softly to Gus. The dog approached. After lifting his paws to the mattress, he hesitated.

"Not you, too," she said. "I'm not sure I can handle being turned down twice in one night."

Gus cocked his head as if considering and then leaped onto the bed. He nosed the quilt for a moment before settling near the foot of the mattress.

Like a small, frightened animal, Everly burrowed under the covers. The blankets smelled of crisp pine and sunshine and the biting cold. They smelled like Wyatt. She inhaled deeply, and Gus began to snore softly. Relaxing into the pillow, Everly stretched out on the bed and her eyes began to feel heavy with sleep.

Wyatt had been right—and he had been wrong. Having Gus in the bed with her made a difference. Wasn't that what she'd wanted from Wyatt—another living and breathing soul to remind Everly that she wasn't alone?

But he'd also been wrong when he said that she didn't want a man as shattered as he was. In fact, Everly imagined that Wyatt wasn't really shattered, not like a broken mirror that was fractured into thousands of pieces. Rather he was an antique-looking glass, veined and faded with disuse. She dropped into a deep well of sleep, floating endlessly until she came upon a mirror. There was something familiar about it. Large. Rectangular. Mounted to a wall. Then she remembered—it was in the hotel, in Axl's room.

Behind Everly stood a figure. She looked at the face in the reflection. The eyes. The nose. The mouth. All the features were clear as crystal.

She sat up, her pulse racing. She gripped the sheets, her fingers winding in and out of the fabric. The dream had been terrifying for sure, but what bothered Everly the most was the realization that she'd seen the killer. And as she'd awakened, the face disappeared into the shadowy corners of her memory.

Chapter 7

In the morning, Wyatt was anxious to get started. He'd showered early and eaten a bowl of cereal—pretty much all he had around resembling breakfast. Everly was also up before the dawn and had showered and eaten early, as well. They knew that today would be monumental for them both. Despite the restless energy that coursed through his veins, he had to get Gus out of the house for a long walk. Besides, there was something else that Wyatt needed to do for Everly.

He was glad to see that she'd dressed for the weather. Jeans. Sweater. Shearling-lined boots. Coat. Hat. Gloves. They strolled through the woods. Dappled sunlight illuminated the blanket of sparkling snow, disturbed only by Gus's paw prints.

Wyatt cast a sideways glance at Everly. Despite her casual clothes, she was still the warrior goddess, but today she was serene—and sad.

Perhaps he could help.

"In town yesterday," he began, "you asked me for help. Asked me to show you where your brother was found. I turned you down on both counts."

"You're helping now. That's all the matters."

Was it? "I can help in other ways, if you want."

She quirked up one eyebrow. "Oh?"

"If you want, I can show you the old schoolhouse. That's where I found your brother."

Everly's pace never faltered. "Okay."

Ever since he'd met her, Everly could be fast, furious, passionate—like a force of nature. But today, she seemed fragile—breakable. Or maybe she was already broken.

Was she offended the he didn't stay in the room last night? It wasn't that Wyatt was an animal, unable to control his basest needs. It's just that where Everly was concerned, he'd have a hell of a time reining himself in.

"Maybe we should talk about last night," he said.

"I had a dream," she began. She kept walking, head down, arms folded. "It was about the killer. I looked in a mirror and I saw their reflection. More than that, I don't think it was simply a dream but actually a memory."

Wyatt stopped in his tracks. Despite the cold, he began to perspire. So, Everly had seen the killer. It just took a bit of sleep to bring that important detail to the surface. He'd seen it happen before in other cases, it's just that he hadn't dared to hope that Everly's memory would resurface.

Wyatt's mind was working out the problem of how to identify someone from sleep. It'd take a good bit of doing. He began to think out loud. "I can find a sketch artist and then we can enter the likeness into a national database of violent offenders."

She shook her head. "Sorry," she said. "I can't…"

"What do you mean?" he asked interrupting.

"I can't remember what they look like, that's the problem," she said, sounding frustrated. "I keep replaying the dream in my mind, but when I look in the mirror, there's nothing there—only a shadow."

Damn. They were so close. "Memories are tricky things," he said. "The harder you try to force the recall, the more it slips through your fingers."

"You seem very calm for someone who's been chasing the same killer for the better part of a decade."

Wyatt placed his hand on his chest. "I'm glad I look serene, but I'm not. My heart is racing and the killer's so close I can almost smell him in the air."

Everly drew in a deep breath, as if trying to catch the scent.

"That memory's in your mind," he said. "Something will trigger it. It'll come back."

"What if it doesn't?" she asked.

"It will," said Wyatt. "Until then, we have other ways to investigate your brother's death." The trail wound around a hill and ascended to a field in the middle of the forest. Mist, rising from the melting snow, surrounded a single dwelling. "We're here," he said, pointing to the old schoolhouse. "That's where I discovered Axl's body."

For a single agonizing moment, the call about Axl's death was more real than the biting air and the distant mountains. Everly had walking out of her apartment, barely on time for a staff meeting. She'd only taken the call because of the Wyoming area code and knowing that her brother was working in the state for the next few weeks. She had expected to hear his voice. Never before had she been more wrong.

"Everly Baker? This is Sheriff Carl Haak of Pleasant Pines, Wyoming. I'm afraid I have some terrible news. It seems there's been an accident."

At that moment, her life had been irrevocably altered. Less than two days later and she had only the haziest recollection of the hours that followed. Somehow, she had the wherewithal to fly to Cheyenne and rent a car—deciding along the way that Axl's death hadn't been accidental and she was determined to find justice for her brother.

Now, she was here—bruised and battered. All the same, she no closer to discovering the truth.

Her throat burned. Her chest ached. A sob bubbled up in her middle and she bit her lip to keep it from breaking free.

"Tell me," she said, her voice hoarse. A single tear rolled down her cheek and she swiped it away with the back of her hand. "Tell me everything you remember about that morning."

Wyatt scratched the side of his face. It was a gesture she'd seen before—his way of buying time while he decided what to do or say next. "It was Gus. We were out on our morning walk. He went after a stick, then ran off and started barking. I just followed."

Walking toward the building, Wyatt left tracks in the snow. Everly followed. Two strands of plastic police tape blocked the doorway. Wyatt stopped at the threshold and Everly stood by his side. "The body, I mean your brother, was in the back corner. There were gouges on his face, but that was postmortem. In fact, I'd say your brother was fed the alcohol and anti-nausea medicine somewhere else and then was dumped here to die."

"Dumped." The word made her sick. "Like garbage." One day soon, she'd cry and curse life for being unfair, but not now. Losing herself in grief wouldn't accomplish anything for Axl. Everly had to stay focused.

Wyatt ducked under the police tape, entering the old building. Everly was right behind. Even after a century of wind, and snow, and rain, all the walls were intact. As if in a dream, she moved to the corner, the place her brother had been found. Tracing her fingers over the cold floor, she tried to find something of Axl—his soul, his energy, or whatever remained after someone died.

There was nothing and Everly knew that she was truly alone in the world. After a moment, she asked,

"What do you think happened? I know he got drunk one way or another and was left here to die, but do you think he suffered?"

"I doubt he felt anything beyond intoxicated," said Wyatt. "In fact, I'd be surprised if he ever knew that he'd been left in this building."

"Axl was a recovering alcoholic," said Everly. "I wonder why he decided to drink again."

"Maybe the taste was somehow masked," Wyatt suggested. "And he was tricked into drinking too much."

"It's subtle," said Everly.

"It's evil," corrected Wyatt. "And calculating as hell."

"I guess what I want to say is that there's no violence to these deaths. The killer didn't shoot anyone or stab anyone or strangle a single person. It's almost like, 'Oops, you got too drunk. Now, I'm going to leave you outside until you die.' You know?"

Wyatt shook his head. "I think that the cut on your neck paints a different picture."

Picture. "We need to look for Axl's camera," she said, interrupting what else Wyatt was about to say. Maybe her brother had taken a picture of his killer. She rushed to the doorway and stepped into the snow. Spinning in a tight circle, Everly scanned the horizon. There was nothing to see beyond snow and trees.

"I doubt we'll find anything now. Let's come back after the snow melts."

"Unless I'm no longer in Pleasant Pines. Didn't

Sheriff Haak tell me I had to leave town as soon as Axl's body was ready to go back to Chicago?"

"Damn. He did. That means we have a lot to do and not as much time as we need." Wyatt consulted a smartwatch on his wrist. "It's a quarter after eight. We can be in town by nine o'clock and go straight to the Rocky Mountain Justice offices."

It wasn't much of a plan, but it was more than Everly could ever do on her own. "Thanks for bringing me out here," she said as they turned back to Wyatt's house. "In a sad way, I think Axl would've appreciated being left in that old schoolhouse. He loved the outdoors—hated the city." She glanced back once more at the ramshackle building then fell into step next to Wyatt, heading toward a future she could barely comprehend.

It was darkest in the shadows cast by the trees. Beyond, the fresh snow sparkled in the morning sun, like a carpet of diamonds. From this distance, the Darkness could see Wyatt and the woman, but not hear what they said.

From the tree line, the Darkness had watched as they trekked to the final resting place. Or one of them, at least. The Darkness made sure that each spot was sacred. Serene. Wyatt had brought the woman, showing the power of the Darkness.

Hatred bubbled up from deep inside. It was almost as if the woman would defile the inviolability of the place. Still, she was the one who had goaded Wyatt and once again, he was playing the game.

And what a game it was!

The Darkness had dared to enter Wyatt's house and trembled with ecstasy for the risk of it all. It was too damn bad that the plan hadn't worked. But if it had? Ah, just to think of Wyatt's terror when he discovered the woman's corpse.

How many years had it been since the Darkness had first seen Wyatt? He'd been interviewed on television in Las Vegas after the third body had been found. It was then that the Darkness knew that finally a worthy opponent had been found. Handsome. Brave. Smart.

When the public turned on the white knight the Darkness knew it had won. Yet, it wasn't enough for the Darkness to win. It wanted to be known. It wanted to look Wyatt in the eyes and see adulation, admiration and love.

The Darkness watched from the shadows and seethed. There—a flicker of emotion passed across Wyatt's face. What had it been? Tenderness? For who—for the woman? What if Wyatt had started to play the game again and it wasn't to defeat the Darkness, but to provide comfort for the woman?

Had the Darkness been wrong to try and harm her? Had that moment allowed Wyatt to protect her—and become the woman's champion? What if she lured him away and Wyatt stopped playing the game?

That would never do. Never. Never. Never.

"'Thou shalt beat him with the rod, and shalt deliver his soul from hell,'" said the Darkness.

Could Wyatt still be saved? Perhaps. But that would require another sacrifice...

Wyatt parked the truck next to the corner and consulted the piece of paper he had thrown on to the dashboard. Glancing at the two-story Victorian mansion on the edge of the Pleasant Pines business district, he admitted it was hardly what he expected from an outfit that slyly referred to itself as providing "private security." Then again, this inconspicuous home might just provide the perfect camouflage.

He scanned the front stoop for a placard or any kind of sign. There was nothing beyond the house number. Everly sat in the passenger seat and he glanced her way.

"Everything okay?" she asked.

Wyatt turned off the ignition and pocketed his keys. "Let's find out."

They walked up the sidewalk and rang the bell. A sleek, silver intercom had been set into the wall. It squawked with a burst of static for a single second before a woman's voice asked, "May I help you?"

Wyatt looked for a call button, but there was none. He leaned forward. "I'm here to see Marcus Jones."

"Name?"

"Wyatt Thornton," he said. "From the Bureau."

"And?" asked the woman.

Wyatt looked around for a camera and saw none. Obviously, appearances were deceiving. "Everly Baker," he said, leaning toward the intercom and raising his voice. "Marcus met her yesterday at the diner."

Wyatt's first impression that this was nothing more than a home—renovated to office space—was quickly replaced. The high-tech and thorough security employed by Rocky Mountain Justice was impressive.

The woman's disembodied voice came through the intercom. "Look at the camera."

The what? Wyatt didn't see anything.

The lock clicked, leaving the door ajar. "Marcus can see you now," said the woman.

Wyatt pulled open the door and stepped into a foyer. The walls were covered in white paper with a golden paisley pattern, so understated that it was only visible in direct light. There was a chair rail of deep mahogany and a striped paper of maroon completed the walls. The floor was covered in hexagonal tiles of black and white—all a typical look for a Victorian mansion, except for one unmistakable difference. The door leading to the house was reinforced steel, controlled by a keypad lock and screen for facial recognition.

Everly moved close behind Wyatt, her mouth close to his ear. "It looks like something out of a James Bond movie."

Before Wyatt could agree, the door opened with a *whoosh*. Marcus Jones stood on the threshold. He wore jeans, a button-up shirt with light blue stripes and a navy blazer. The classic outfit was at odds with the innovative surroundings. "Hey, Wyatt," said

Jones. He offered his palm. "I didn't think I'd see you again so soon."

Taking the other man's hand to shake, Wyatt said, "I—we—need your help."

"Sure," said Marcus. "What can I do for you?"

"Is there someplace we can talk?" asked Wyatt. "Someplace that's a little more private."

Jones nodded. "Follow me."

They stepped through the metal entrance. A similar keypad and monitor for facial recognition were also attached to the inner door. Marcus tapped out a six-digit code, then stepped up to the scanner. Marcus's likeness appeared on the screen. Twenty identification points were checked. A green light atop the scanner flashed and the door slid open.

There was a curving staircase in front of them and another door at the back of the hall. There were also two wooden doors—one on the left and the other on the right. All of them were shut, the lock controlled with a keypad and scanner.

"That's quite the security setup you have," said Wyatt, half conversationally, half in awe. "What is that you do here again?"

"We do a little bit of everything. Anti-industrial espionage. Security for businesses. Sometimes we help out when local law enforcement needs a hand."

Wyatt was starting to get a picture of the work done by Rocky Mountain Justice. "The government hires you because you don't have to play by the rules and can push boundaries they can't," said Wyatt.

Jones didn't bother answering the question, which was an answer in itself.

"Right now, we're a small crew. Elite, I like to call it," said Jones as he led them up a winding staircase. "RMJ's headquarters are in Denver. We have three operatives in the Wyoming office, myself included, as well as a communications specialist. I'm looking to expand with the right people."

The offer to join the crew was definite. "I appreciate you hearing me out and offering to help," said Wyatt. "But I'm retired."

"Retired?" Jones chuckled. "You sound so old when you say that. How old are you?"

"I'll be thirty-seven in August."

"You've got plenty of years left to work."

"Still not interested," said Wyatt with a shake of his head. Everly had been silent during the exchange and he wondered what she thought about him leaving the work force at such a young age. She had an opinion—he'd bet money on it—if only because she had an opinion on everything.

Then again, why did he care what she thought? He was helping her find justice for her brother—and in turn, he was tying up the biggest loose end of his life. When he thought about it that way, Everly's opinion didn't matter as much.

The staircase ended in the middle of a hallway. Seven doors stretched out along the corridor—three to the right and four to the left.

"This way," Marcus said, pointing to the right. At the second door, Marcus entered yet another code and waited while the facial-identification software ran. The latch automatically released with a click and Marcus turned the handle and opened the door.

It was a computer lab, as sophisticated as any Wyatt had seen in the secure rooms at the Hoover Building or the in bowels of the NSA. Several monitors hung on the wall and even more sat on a semicircular group of tables. There were four keyboards, and a private server hummed at the back of the room.

So, while this incredibly high-tech operation wasn't uncommon at the highest level of the government, it sure as hell was uncommon for a private agency. He doubted that Marcus Jones would give him more information about RMJ than he'd already gotten, but Wyatt was certain he would now have access to any database he needed.

"Have a seat," said Marcus. There were four chairs on wheels and Everly selected one. Wyatt took a seat next to her and Marcus sat near the door. He rested his elbow on the table. "Downstairs you said you wanted to speak privately," he said.

Marcus was like that. He didn't exactly ask questions, just gave openings for information to be given. Yet, what did Wyatt want to say? Marcus had been a special agent in Charge of the Bureau's Denver field office. Even though he'd been part of management, he hadn't worked on the Las Vegas case. He didn't know everything Wyatt did—it was time to bring Jones up to speed.

"This is about the last case I worked," said Wyatt.

"Las Vegas." This was from Marcus. Again, not a question, not a statement.

Wyatt nodded. "The serial killer I was hunting there has resurfaced here in Pleasant Pines."

Jones sucked in a breath and his eyes widened. It was a quick reaction, yet unmistakable. "You have my attention."

"My brother was one of the killer's victims. We think there might be others, but we need access to information in some law enforcement databases." Everly said. "We're hoping you can help us with that search."

"What do you need?" asked Marcus.

Focusing on the important details, Wyatt said, "The killer in Vegas left a calling card of sorts—it was half of a two-dollar bill that was placed in the wallet of all his victims. It's how we first knew all the killings were connected."

"I never heard about that link between the victims."

"It was kept classified. We didn't want any of it leaking to the media and then having to deal with copycat killers."

"I'm guessing that there's a link with this newest death?"

Everly rolled her chair forward an inch. "Half of a two-dollar bill was found in my brother's wallet."

"And the circumstances around the death were similar." Wyatt added, "In Nevada, all the victims had a very high blood-alcohol content and were found in the middle of the desert."

"Several men died of exposure in Pleasant Pines over the past couple of years, just like my brother," Everly continued. "They all had a similarly high blood-alcohol level and had happened to wander into the woods where they died."

"You want to see if those men have half of a two-dollar bill among their possessions?" Marcus asked.

"Exactly," said Wyatt.

"I have to ask—did you take this information to the sheriff?"

"We told him about the two-dollar bill and the connection to Wyatt's old case," said Everly. "But the medical examiner ruled accidental exposure as the cause of death and Sheriff Haak didn't want to listen to what we had to say."

"I know the sheriff kept a record of all the personal belongings found with each body. I also assume a copy's been kept in the database, but without the sheriff giving us access to his computer, we're stuck..." Wyatt let the statement dangle like a hook in the water, and he hoped like hell that Marcus would take a bite.

"Which is why you came here," said Marcus.

"Pretty much," Wyatt said.

Marcus swiveled toward the table and began tapping on a keyboard. The RMJ site filled one of the monitors on the wall. "Let's see what we can find out about these recent deaths." The sheriff's office site came up and within seconds, they had accessed a private page.

"Is this legal?" Everly whispered.

Marcus held up his hand, tilting it from side to side. *So-so.*

Wyatt's gaze was drawn to the computer's cursor. His pulse grew stronger with each beat until the steady *thump, thump* echoed in his skull. "See if you can find a master list for property located on recently deceased."

Marcus typed, and another field appeared.

"Try *half of a two-dollar bill*," he said.

Marcus didn't hesitate and entered the phrase into the search engine. A colorful ball spun for a minute and stopped. *Your query has four matches.* There were four names listed, as well. Wyatt picked up a notepad and pen from the table and scribbled them down. "Robert Barnes. Jeffery Stone. Brian Green. Seth Carlson."

"So, what do we do now?" Everly asked. "Go to the sheriff?"

She looked from Wyatt to Marcus and back again.

It was Marcus who answered. "There's at least some proof that four other men were found with half of a two-dollar bill on their person. It's a lot more than a coincidence if you ask me. More than that, it should warrant some kind of investigation."

Wyatt folded his arms across his chest. With a shake of his head, he said, "It's still thin. We need to know as much as we can about the other guys—see if there are connections beside the obvious."

"Gender. Place of death. The torn-up money." Marcus counted out the facts as he spoke. "That's more than a little thin."

"If this is a serial killer—" Wyatt began.

"If?" Marcus interrupted. "If? I thought you were sure, that's why you came here. Why the sudden change of heart?"

"I keep coming back to the same question—why? What's his motivation? Why does he need to kill these men?"

"Plain and simple," said Everly. "He has his own agenda, even if nothing he does makes sense to us."

"That's where you're wrong. Serial killers are highly intelligent and very methodical. There's always a reason for everything they do. More than that, every case that I'd worked before this one had another common theme. All the killers fed off the terror of their victims."

He continued. "They liked knowing the other person was in pain and feared for their life. This morning, Everly pointed out that there's no viciousness to any of these killings. Aside from the calling card, each death looks natural."

"Maybe he's a new breed of serial killer," Marcus suggested.

Wyatt lifted one shoulder and let it drop. The scenario didn't fit. Or rather, it was too perfect of a fit. So why the hesitation? Was there something wrong with his theory? Or was he paralyzed by the past, afraid to make another mistake that might ruin him once and for all?

Chapter 8

Everly and Wyatt had spent the better part of two hours tracing the life of each of the victims. Marcus Jones stayed with them for the first hour but left when he received a phone call from RMJ's headquarters in Denver.

While consulting the notepad in front of her, Everly said, "The similarities in all these men are eerie."

"They were all from out of state, visiting for work or waiting for friends—and therefore by themselves." Wyatt shifted in his seat. "The fact that they were alone made them easy targets. No one to miss them when they first disappeared."

Had Axl been an easy target? Everly hated to think that somehow her brother had been exploited.

A shard of grief stabbed her in the chest. She bit her lip. The pain was cleansing.

"I'm sorry if what I said sounds callous. I guess sometimes I can come across a little academic," he said.

How was it that Wyatt could read her so well? Oh, yeah—he was a behavioral scientist and she'd be wise not to see something special about his attentiveness.

"I'm okay," she said with a shake of her head. "You're right. Axl was alone and he was an alcoholic years ago. He went to treatment, and maybe thinking he could control his addiction left him more susceptible to being..." Everly couldn't bring herself to finish the thought, much less the sentence.

"Do you want to take a break?" Wyatt asked. "This has been tough on you."

"A break from what?" She laughed, and her voice cracked. "Finding out who killed my brother is the only thing that matters to me right now. Or might ever matter again."

"Let's wrap this up then," said Wyatt as he let go of her wrist. "Let's go over everything we've found so far."

She paused. "Each man in this list is almost exactly the same. Sure, their hometowns were different, as were the reasons they were in Pleasant Pines—but they were all the same, down to their approximate height, weight and coloring. It's as if the killer has a type."

Wyatt leaned back in his chair and cradled his

head in his hands. "Like I said earlier, a serial killer is obsessed with having the same kind of victim. Basically, the killer is recreating an event from their past. What they need is new people, similar looking people, to replay the same role again and again."

"Unfortunately," said Everly, "my brother was a perfect fit." She waited a beat. "How have these deaths not been connected? How is it that no one ever figured out that four men have been murdered by the same person?"

"Look at the dates," he said. "While it's becoming obvious to us now, those dots are pretty far apart for anyone who's not looking to create a picture. Still, years ago, I had a team of two dozen agents and more than twice that number of police officers dedicated to finding the killer. Even with all those resources, we never figured out who was responsible."

Before Wyatt could say more, Everly's phone began to ring. She fished it from her bag. "It's Sheriff Haak," she said. "Axl's body is probably ready to be taken back to Chicago, which means I need to get out of town."

"Put the call on speakerphone and tell him I'm here. He may not agree to open an investigation now, but I think we can get him to meet with us."

Everly swiped the speaker icon before setting the phone on the table. "Sheriff Haak," she said. "I'm here with Wyatt Thornton." How many business meetings had Everly taken in the same manner? So many that the words felt comfortable and yet, this phone call wasn't about anything as mundane as an advertising campaign or a client's public-relations problem.

"Oh, really?" the sheriff said, his tone brittle.

Wyatt leaned toward the phone and spoke. "I'm sure you remember that I found a link between the death of Axl Baker and an old case of mine."

"I do remember," said the sheriff, "and I'm sure you can recall that I told you there was no way in hell that a serial killer was loose in Pleasant Pines."

"I know you've been in law enforcement for years," said Wyatt. "I trust your instincts, but we've done a little digging of our own and have a total of five men who've died over the past three years—all of them died due to a combination of alcohol poisoning and exposure."

"I'd say you went digging in the wrong place. The number of those types of accidental deaths is likely three times as high. This is Wyoming. People go hunting and twist an ankle, making it impossible to get back. They go skiing and lose the trail. Hell, sometimes they just go outside, and a blizzard catches them unawares. Do you want me to continue?" asked the sheriff. Everly could imagine the older man sitting in his office, finger stabbing the desk as his face grew redder and redder with rage and frustration.

Wyatt continued, the pulse at the base of his neck thrummed with the urgency of his words. "Each man was in his early to mid-thirties, from out of town, visiting alone—or waiting for his group to arrive. The cause of death was exactly the same."

"Anything else?" asked Sheriff Haak, his voice small.

"And," Wyatt continued, "each man was found with half of a two-dollar bill in his wallet."

Sheriff Haak didn't respond, yet the seconds of the call ticked by.

"I know how much you care about this town," Everly said. It was time for her to contribute and do her job. "I know you've dedicated your life to keeping everyone in Pleasant Pines safe, but there's too much evidence to ignore." She paused, waiting for the sheriff, or even Wyatt, to add something to the conversation. Neither did, so she continued. "I've been attacked twice since arriving in Pleasant Pines and started asking questions about Axl. It's hard to believe that those are random events and not meant to scare me into leaving town."

"Why's this the first time I'm hearing about you being attacked?" the sheriff asked.

"You haven't been interested in seeing Axl Baker's death from another angle," said Wyatt. "We needed more information before speaking to you again."

"Can we meet with you? We can be at your office in a few minutes," said Everly.

"I'll hear you out," said the sheriff, "but not at my office. The county building is a busy place with folks coming and going all day. I don't want any of your theories being overheard and needlessly frightening anyone." He sighed.

"Obviously," said Wyatt, "we'd be discreet."

"I can't use my place," said the sheriff. "We have contractors working in the office. It's too chaotic."

"Where then?" Everly asked.

"There is no discretion in my office, trust me."

The line was filled with a moment of silence. Finally, the sheriff said, "There's a conference room we sometimes use at the Pleasant Pines Inn for training and such. At this hour it'll be empty and private. Meet me there in twenty minutes."

Everly exchanged a glance with Wyatt. A conference room at a hotel? How secure could that be? All the same, she wasn't well-versed in small-town American law enforcement. *Maybe this is just how it's done here*, she thought. Scooping up her notepad, Everly said, "We'll be there."

"Before you go," said the sheriff, "I have one question. How'd you know that the men were found with half of a two-dollar bill?"

Wyatt answered. "An old friend of mine works for Rocky Mountain Justice. He let me access databases from his office."

"I don't know what Rocky Mountain Justice is, so you need to bring him, too," said the sheriff. "I have lots of questions and if I don't like the answers I get, there's going to be hell to pay."

The conference room was located on the first floor of the inn, just a space tucked off of the now closed restaurant. Darcy, the desk clerk, had been overly helpful when they arrived. She arranged the room for the meeting, bringing water bottles, a tray of sandwiches, and pads of paper emblazoned with the Pleasant Pines Inn logo. By the time Sheriff Haak appeared, Everly, Wyatt and Marcus were fully prepared to brief the local lawman.

Since then, more than an hour had passed. The water bottles were empty, and the tray only held crumbs.

Everly sat at the circular table with Wyatt on her left and Marcus on her right. Sheriff Haak sat directly across from her. His sheriff's hat, with the tin star on the band, rested on the table in front of him.

Wyatt had just finished going through all the connections between the local deaths, Axl Baker and his former case from Las Vegas, painting a grisly picture. Wyatt concluded with "That's why I'm convinced that Pleasant Pines has become the hunting grounds for this murderer."

Running his fingers over the brim of his hat, Sheriff Haak asked, "This is your professional opinion, Mister G-man?"

Wyatt ignored the comment and tapped a pen on the table. "It is."

Sheriff Haak turned to Marcus Jones. "What about you? What do you think?"

"I think that Wyatt Thornton is as fine an agent as there is," he said. "This information is real—and you need to open a full investigation into these killings."

The sheriff's cheeks turned a blotchy red. He obviously took a great deal of pride in his community. Moreover, Everly guessed that he didn't welcome anyone telling him how to do his job. Nor did he want to be accused of having missed something so important as a serial killer in his town. If pushed too hard, she knew that the sheriff would push back.

"Sheriff Haak," she said. "I don't have experience in this kind of thing, like the three of you. But I do want to know what happened to my brother. Believe me, I wish his death was a simple accident, as you originally told me. But that's not the case. No one is accusing you of being a second-rate sheriff. If you don't look into these cases now and find out what's really going on, the whole town will be at risk. You're too good of a man to do that," she said.

With a grunt, the sheriff asked, "What do you know about the killer?"

"Typically, the profile for most serial killers is similar," said Wyatt, nonplussed, as usual. "They tend to be Caucasian, highly intelligent and in their late twenties to early thirties."

"Is that always true?" asked Sheriff Haak.

Wyatt said, "No, not always. Maybe eighty-five percent of serial killers are Caucasian men. Some can be people of color. Even fewer serial killers are female. During the initial investigation in Vegas we assumed that the killer fit the most basic profile. There was never any evidence to prove otherwise."

Wyatt continued. "Because of the simple mode of killing, we doubt that the killer has much more than a high-school education but is intelligent. He is most likely manipulative or, at the very least, charming. Leaving half of a two-dollar bill with each victim, I believe, represents a broken promise. In Vegas, we suspected a hospitality worker."

"Any old hospitality worker, or a specific one?" the sheriff asked.

Everly knew the answer to this question. In Las Vegas, Wyatt had accused a blackjack dealer and the man had been arrested. Later, an alibi was established for the suspect, and Wyatt's career had been left in tatters. It wasn't a fact he'd confessed to her and it left Everly wondering what Wyatt would say.

"We arrested a man who worked in a hotel casino on the Strip. Not all the facts fit, and he was let go," said Wyatt. "After that, the killings stopped, and then local law enforcement took over. There were never any other arrests and to this day, case is cold."

"What you're telling me is that you don't have a clue," said the sheriff.

"I still believe the killer worked in the service industry. We just had the wrong guy in Vegas."

"That makes sense. There's a connection to this inn," said Marcus. "All the victims have been guests here."

"This is the only place in town," said the sheriff. "It's not like visitors have much of a choice."

"But they were here," said Marcus, his fingers splayed across the table. "It's also the last place any of them were seen alive."

"That has to be a clue worth something," Everly said.

"It's worth a lot more than something," said Wyatt.

"Especially since we found a link. Axl Baker had an argument with a cook at the hotel—Larry Walker."

"I know Larry," said the sheriff. "What'd they argue about?"

"I'm not sure," said Everly. "The bartender overheard them having a heated discussion. From what she said, it had to do with what my brother was here to photograph."

"It might do for us to have a chat with Larry and see what he remembers about Axl," said Marcus.

"Larry fits your profile from the Nevada case," the sheriff said to Wyatt. "Down to the age, educational level and employment. He was even a troubled kid—fights at school, running away when he got mad at his mother and the like. He's no charmer, though. Larry was born and raised here, but he left five or six years ago to find work. Came back less than three years past."

"Not too many months before the first victim was killed," said Wyatt.

"It might do to ask Larry more than what he remembers about Axl Baker, but what he knows about all of these men," Marcus suggested.

"I agree," said Sheriff Haak. "I'll bring him in and officially question him about all of these deaths…"

His statement was followed by a clattering in the hallway. Metal clanged against metal and the sound of shattering glass screeched. Everly's heartbeat hammered against her chest and she swiveled in her chair toward the sound. A lanky man with sparse dark hair and a high forehead stood in the doorway, with an oval tray in his hands. A coffeepot, broken cups, spoons and saucers littered the floor at his feet.

He stared into the room with a wide-eyed gaze. The tray wobbled on his hand before toppling from his precarious grasp with a clang. With a final, wild-eyed look the man turned and sprinted from view.

On their feet in the same instant, Wyatt and Marcus rushed from the room. Their footfalls were thunder in the small space.

Then they were gone, and silence followed.

Everly turned to the sheriff. "Who was that?" she asked.

Haak shook his head. "That was Larry Walker. Your prime suspect."

Wyatt's heart hammered against his chest, his breath resonating in his skull. His footsteps slapped on the floor of the cramped hallway. Marcus was just a step behind. But Wyatt wasn't concerned about who followed. Rather, he was focused on who was in front.

He'd never met Larry Walker, yet Wyatt would bet good money that he was the man they now chased. Wyatt reached out and his fingers touched the fabric of a sleeve. He tried to grab hold, but the man slipped from his grasp.

Daylight erupted into the dark corridor, the glare blinding, as the man pushed the side door and exited. Wyatt's speed carried him forward a pace or two, then he skidded to a stop. He pivoted and burst through the same door.

He was in a parking lot, half-full and covered in gravel. Larry was a full ten yards away. The lights on a small pickup truck flashed and the engine revved as Larry used a key fob to engage the remote starter. Larry was already halfway to the truck. And if he got there before Wyatt got to him, he knew the suspect would disappear—and it would be hell to find him.

Wyatt had only one chance. He caught up and dove forward, grabbing the other man around the middle. They tumbled to the ground, coming to a stop with Wyatt pinning Larry facedown. Gravel gouged his flesh and scraped his skin raw. Wyatt cared nothing for the pain.

Larry clawed at him, trying to escape, but Wyatt grabbed the other man's arm and tore the key fob from his grasp. He stood slowly and turned off the truck. The motor fell silent. Wyatt's labored breathing was the only thing he heard.

Marcus approached. He'd drawn a sidearm and was pointing it directly at Larry. "Hold your hands where I can see them," Marcus ordered.

Larry lifted his palms. A tremor shook his arms. "Come on, what'd you want, man?"

"We need to talk," said Wyatt.

"Talk if you want, but you don't need to point that gun at me. I didn't do nothing wrong."

"If you didn't do anything wrong, why did you run?"

"Because a room full of cops was talking about me in connection with the dead guy," said Larry.

"If you were in my place and had any sense, you'd run, too."

"On your feet," Marcus ordered. "I think we need to have a little chat with the sheriff."

Hands still lifted, Larry walked back to the conference room. Marcus was directly behind Larry, with Wyatt bringing up the rear. Once in the conference room, Marcus gestured to a chair with the barrel of his gun. "Sit," he said.

Larry took a seat and turned to the sheriff. "What the hell's going on? Those two chased me down. That one—" he pointed to Wyatt "—took the keys to my truck. And the other one pulled a piece on me. I can sue for this. I have rights, you know."

"Shut up, Larry," said the sheriff.

Larry fell silent.

Marcus slid his gun into a holster on his ankle and sat. Wyatt took a seat as well, choosing one directly across from Larry.

"We need to ask you a few questions," said Wyatt.

"I don't have to answer anything," said Larry. "I know my rights."

"You don't have to say anything here," said the sheriff. "Even more than that, you aren't under arrest. This is a friendly conversation, but if you don't want to talk, I can take you to my office and things will work out different."

Larry rolled his hand. "Fine. We can talk."

"What do you know about Axl Baker?" Wyatt asked.

Larry pulled his eyebrows together. "Who?"

"Axl Baker," said Everly. "My brother. You argued with him at the bar and then his body was found the next morning."

"That's bad luck, man," said Larry.

For the first time, Wyatt saw yellow sweat stains on Larry's shirt at the underarms and neck. He also noticed how they'd become damp again as the other man perspired. He nervously folded his hands together and unfolded them, moving constantly. Signs of discomfort were uncommon for sociopaths, the likes of which had been killing people for years.

"Whose bad luck?" asked Wyatt. "Axl's or yours?"

"Both, I guess," said Larry.

"Tell me what happened the other night," said Wyatt.

"Nothing," said Larry.

From years of training, Wyatt knew that the best way to get information was to wait. A subject with ample time and too much silence would eventually fill both with what they assumed an investigator wanted to hear. Eventually, it would lead to the truth. Too bad Wyatt didn't have the patience to wait for Larry to talk in circles. "Don't screw with me," he said. "I'm not in the mood."

Larry looked at the sheriff and then back at Wyatt. "We argued a little, it's no big deal."

"What'd you argue about?"

"Nothing."

Wyatt slapped the table, the sound causing everyone to jump. Larry leaned back, his eyes went wide. "Let's assume it's not nothing."

"It really wasn't anything important. The Baker guy wanted to track wolf migration. I told him that the wolves weren't for his amusement. He said that he was on an assignment, trying to do a job to educate people. I didn't care. Things got a little heated and voices were raised. That's all."

Sheriff Haak asked, "Why were you listening at the door?"

"Darcy told me to bring some coffee to this meeting. I was about to knock but heard my name." Larry shrugged. "I eavesdropped a little, I guess."

It explained the shattered coffeepot and broken cups.

"Where were you the night before last?"

"Come on, Sheriff," said Larry, his tone wheedling. "You aren't going to let them question me like this, are you? I have the right to my privacy."

"If you have nothing to hide, then answer the questions," said Sheriff Haak.

Larry cursed under his breath and wiped a hand across the back of his neck. "The kitchen closed around nine o'clock. I cleaned up and came out for a drink. That Baker guy started chatting me up. Had I always lived in Pleasant Pines? What did I know about the wolves? I just wanted my drink and to relax. His constant questions were annoying, and I said something. Johanna said I couldn't fight with the customers and told me to go home. I did, and it was quarter after ten when I walked out of the inn."

"Wife? Family? Roommates?" asked Marcus. "Anyone who could corroborate your story?"

Larry shook his head. "I live alone in an apartment two blocks away."

"What about last night?" Wyatt asked. He had a hard time imagining Larry Walker breaking into his home much less thinking to barricade the door and then getting away. But, if Larry was the killer, then he'd done just that. "Where were you?"

"Home by ten thirty. No arguments in the bar, so I got to finish my drink."

"I have one more question," said Wyatt.

"No." Larry held up his hands and waved away the probe. "No more questions. I haven't done anything wrong and I'm not going to be treated like a criminal. I don't have an alibi for the night that Baker was killed, but unless you're going to arrest me, Sheriff, I'm leaving."

"Consider yourself a person of interest in this case, Larry," said Sheriff Haak. "Don't leave town or I'll issue a warrant for your arrest and throw you in jail."

"For what?" Larry asked.

"For killing Axl Baker," the sheriff said.

After cursing under his breath, Larry said, "I need the keys to my truck." He pointed to Wyatt. "That guy took them."

"Go ahead, Mr. Thornton. Give them back," said the sheriff.

Wyatt uttered a curse of his own as he fished them from his jeans and slid them across the table. Larry scooped up the keys and shoved them into his pocket.

"This is total crap," said Larry as he stood. His

chair teetered back before toppling and clattering to the ground. Larry kicked it out of the way, then stalked to the door and disappeared into the hallway.

"Let me handle this," said Marcus Jones as he got to his feet. "I'll keep an eye on Larry for now."

"I'll be in touch," said Wyatt before the other man left.

Everly folded her arms tightly across her chest. She glared at the sheriff, her green eyes flashing with incredulity. "Are you kidding me? You're just going to let Larry go? You heard him—he doesn't have an alibi for the night my brother was killed. Or last night, when I was attacked. He works in the hotel, which means he might've attacked me yesterday morning, as well."

"Now might be a good time to tell me about the attacks you just mentioned."

Everly caught the sheriff up to speed on everything that had happened, not leaving out any details. As she finished, she said, "You can't just let Larry go."

"Unfortunately, we don't throw people in to jail without a reason," said Haak. "He was voluntarily answering the questions we asked, and his answers make enough sense that I'm not placing him in custody. But, I am putting him under twenty-four/seven surveillance. If he tries to leave town, we'll know."

"Is that it?" asked Everly. Her tone dripped with the same skepticism that Wyatt felt.

Wyatt clenched his jaw. To Haak, he said, "I want a murder investigation opened. We need a search warrant to get into Larry's apartment *now,* before he disposes of any evidence. Or worse, skips town and we never see him again."

"Why don't you give me all of the evidence you've collected?" suggested the sheriff. "I'll review everything again."

With only two weeks left on the job, Wyatt wondered how diligent the sheriff would be with any new investigation. That meant it was up to Wyatt, and hell would freeze over before he gave Haak any information he collected. "That's not good enough," he said.

"I've said this before, and I'll say it again—I've kept this town safe for decades. I'm not going to get everyone into a panic for no reason, especially since I only have a few weeks on the job."

"I get it," Wyatt said. "You don't want to sully your reputation with an at-large serial killer, not when you're retiring in a few days."

"That's a harsh criticism and I won't have it," said the sheriff. "This town has been my life and I won't have you two show up and cause an upheaval for a lot of people."

Wyatt wasn't certain if he should believe the sheriff or not. Either way, he decided that that lawman was irrelevant. Besides, wasn't it working with a team that had ruined Wyatt's career all those years ago?

"Tell you what," said Wyatt. "I'm going to keep looking into this case. Because I know we're on the right track."

"Do what you have to do," the sheriff said. "I will

get a deputy to follow Larry around like I promised." Haak stood slowly and picked up his hat. "In fact, I'll see to it now."

The sheriff left the room and it was Wyatt's turn to be pinned by Everly's fiery stare. "What was that all about?" she asked. "Are you just going to let the sheriff ignore the facts? I thought you wanted the serial killer brought to justice."

Wyatt sighed. "Haak is a decent man, but he's old and has some misguided notion of needing a legacy." He continued, "Or maybe he's just tired. Either way, it's obvious that he's not going to give this investigation the attention it needs."

"And you will?" asked Everly, finishing Wyatt's sentence for him.

It was exactly what he'd planned. In fact, this was a perfect scenario—Wyatt's continued investigation had been given the blessing of a disinterested sheriff. Along with his expertise and the resources of RMJ, Wyatt would have the chance to rewrite history. To catch the killer and erase the stain on his career. Hell, on his life. Like an electric current under his skin, Wyatt itched to begin the hunt.

"Will you give the investigation all the attention it needs?" Everly asked, repeating her question.

Giving a noncommittal shrug, Wyatt asked, "Why is that a problem?"

"It depends," she said.

The room was silent, save for the beating of Wyatt's heart and the whisper of Everly's breath. His skin suddenly felt too tight. "It depends on what?"

"On whether you plan on having me help—or not. Because you aren't getting rid of me, Wyatt Thornton. I won't rest until my brother gets justice."

Wyatt didn't hate the idea of Everly staying around for a few more days. And the fact that Wyatt wanted Everly to stay with him was the biggest danger of all.

Chapter 9

Everly sat at the computer desk in Wyatt's living room. A fire burned in the hearth and the late-afternoon sun shone through the windows. They had once again found a copy of Larry Walker's criminal history and the computer glowed with a litany of misdeeds.

"Here's what we know," said Wyatt. "Larry Walker doesn't fit the textbook definition of a serial killer. Serial killers are sly and cunning. Larry Walker is the human equivalent of a bullhorn."

"But he is a violent man, who happened to fight with Axl the night he died. He also had access to all of the other victims," she said. "Besides, he fits your initial profile—age, gender, ethnicity."

"True, but there are a lot of crimes on his rap sheet and none of them are close to murder."

"There's a progression of violence. Troubled kid. Drugs. Larceny. Assault. Jumping to murder isn't a big leap."

Wyatt paused and she knew that she'd scored a point.

After a moment, he spoke. "If Larry were to kill someone, it'd be in a fit of rage. A shot to the head over a woman or a fistfight gone awry."

Everly sucked in a breath. "What is it that you're trying to do, Wyatt? Prove that Larry isn't guilty?"

He shook his head. "Look, I'm covering my tracks. I was wrong about a suspect before. I'm not going to be wrong again." He sighed. "More even than the profile not matching perfectly, is that fact that there's no direct link between Larry and any of the victims—here or in Las Vegas—other than your brother. Without that, we'll have a hell of a time proving that he's guilty."

"So, what do we do? Go back to RMJ and use their equipment?"

"We could," said Wyatt. "Sometimes all a case needs is some old-school investigating. I have a buddy with the Las Vegas Police Department. He owes me a favor. Now might be the time to cash in."

He placed a call on his cell. Turning on the speaker, Wyatt set the phone on the desk. After the third ring, a man's voice came over the line. "This is Davis."

"Davis, this is Wyatt Thornton," he said.

"*Wyatt?* Where the hell have you been, man? I

never thought that I'd hear from you again, not after how it ended here."

"I'm...not with the Bureau anymore. Actually, because of how things went down, but that's why I'm calling. Some information has come my way about that case, and I was hoping I could call in a favor."

"You know I owe you, man. Ask away."

"Can you run a name for me? Lawrence or Larry Walker." Wyatt added in Larry's birthdate. "I need residences. Places of employment. Anything you got."

"That might be too big of a favor," said Davis. He paused a beat and added, "Without a reason, at least."

"A body turned up in Pleasant Pines, Wyoming. The circumstances are similar to Las Vegas."

"Similar how?" Davis asked.

Wyatt paused. Could he trust Davis? All the same, there was a more important question he knew that he should be asking. What was the likelihood that Davis would help without the facts?

"Two-dollar bill, ripped in half, in the victim's wallet. High BAC. No other trauma. Good looking Caucasian male," said Wyatt, running down the list.

Davis cursed. "Same thing we had here."

"That's exactly what I thought."

"Without a warrant this would have to be on the down-low," said Davis. "But you knew that already. Is this the best number to call?"

"It is," said Wyatt. "And thanks."

"Don't thank me yet," said Davis. "I haven't given you any information."

The line beeped and went dead.

"Now what do we do?" she asked. "Wait?"

"There's not much more we can do now."

"This sucks," she said.

His palm rested on the desk, and he inched closer, his fingers grazed hers. Everly's breath caught.

It was such a simple gesture, barely a touch, but it made her pulse race, and her body throb with heat. It was futile to lie—even to herself. The small caress of his fingers held the promise of much, much more.

Was that really what Everly wanted? To lose herself in Wyatt's arms…? To feel his lips on her mouth? To burn with desire as his touch scorched her skin? To savor the breathless moment when he entered her fully?

Then again, could she really get tangled up with her emotions when the only thing she should be focusing on was finding her brother's killer?

Like ice had been poured into her veins, Everly froze. She pulled her hand away and moved to the window seat. Placing her palms on the sill, she stared at the jagged Rocky Mountains in the distance. The sky had turned to rose and violet. The distant peaks were black in the waning light.

Everly longed to fall into Wyatt's arms and let him take away all of her worries, even if it was for a single night. But that would be a terrible mistake. He was helping her find Axl's killer. How would they navigate their tenuous partnership if they slept together?

A sob escaped her throat. She couldn't believe

she'd let herself be distracted by thoughts of something like sex. Tears streamed down her cheeks. She scrubbed her face. "I'm sorry," she said. "I don't know why I'm crying."

"Because," said Wyatt, "you've been through a lot of trauma in a few short days. Your brother's been killed. You were attacked. This is a lot to take on."

Sad didn't seem a large enough word for Everly's emotions. She was filled with rage and hatred and despair and loneliness and anguish and, yes, sadness. "Axl was a real wanderer. He traveled all over the country—he'd go anywhere for work, really loved his job. Just going from one assignment to the next. But I always knew that eventually he'd come home. Now? That'll never happen again."

"Do you have other family?"

She shook her head. "Our parents died when I was a junior in college in a car crash. Axl was in art school and moved back to Chicago just so I could come home over breaks. He always looked out for me."

Wyatt took a seat next to Everly and wrapped an arm around her shoulder. He pulled her to him, and she leaned into the embrace. The tears seemed endless, but eventually the crying stopped. Everly let Wyatt hold her.

Originally, Everly had sought out Wyatt for his expertise. It was a decision that had been driven by desperation and fear.

What would happen if she stayed—enveloped in Wyatt's embrace?

"Do you think it's safe for me to go back into town and try staying at the inn tonight?"

"No," he said simply. "I don't. Not while the killer is still at large. In fact, I don't really think it's safe for you anywhere."

A trace of his breath tickled her cheek. Everly knew she should move away, and yet, she was rooted to the spot. "I mean, since our prime suspect is being watched by the police, he can't exactly attack me again."

"I hate to say it, but having him under surveillance isn't foolproof. You hope that the subject doesn't sneak away," said Wyatt. He shook his head. "More than that, what if Larry isn't guilty? That means someone else is the killer. Someone outside our surveillance."

"I don't want to die," she said. Everly was exhausted. She turned to the window, pressing her palms onto the glass.

"Then stay," he offered. Wyatt moved closer, shoulder-to-shoulder, and placed his hand next to hers.

"Stay, and then what?" she asked.

"Stay with me. I'll keep you safe."

Yes, that's what she wanted—needed. In Wyatt's arms, Everly could pretend that the world was safe and beautiful. It would be a lie, but it was her lie— and certainly no one would get hurt by her small fib.

Everly studied Wyatt in the reflective glass. His image looked worn, faded—like a ghost. Yet she knew all too well that he was flesh and blood. A steady pulse rose and fell in the hollow of his throat. She reached out again, surer this time, and placed her palm over Wyatt's hand.

His gaze dropped to where they were connected. She slid her fingers between his and closed the space between them. She pressed her breasts into his hard chest and rose up on tiptoe to lick the seam of his lips. He wrapped an arm around her waist and pulled her hard, drawing Everly in closer still. She gave a gasp of surprise and Wyatt placed his lips on hers.

Wyatt slipped his tongue into her mouth. Everly opened herself as he explored, tasted, conquered. And she was in the mood to be taken captive.

He sat her on the window seat and tilted her back. Cold from the glass seeped through her sweater and chilled her flesh. The heat from Wyatt's body was scalding. Ice and fire. Wyatt lifted the fabric of Everly's sweater up inch by inch, and she shivered with anticipation. Her nipples were already hard, and he stroked them through the silky fabric of her bra.

"Wyatt," she breathed, unable to think of anything beyond the man who claimed her with his touch and kisses.

He broke away, his eyes searching her face. His eyebrows were drawn together. "Are you okay?" he asked.

She was trembling. "I'm fine."

"These past few days have been a lot for you," he said. "I doubt that you're fine."

"What are you saying?"

"I'm saying that we won't do anything you don't want to. I don't want to take advantage because of this situation you're in."

She raked her fingers through his hair and jerked his head back, exposing his throat. Everly ran her tongue over his flesh, tasting the salt of his skin. "I'm no china doll," she said. "I won't break."

Wyatt gave a low growl of desire. "I can see that."

"I want you, Wyatt."

Wyatt's hand traveled to Everly's rear. He squeezed. "Is this what you want?" he asked. His grip tightened. The front of his jeans pressed against her. He was hard.

"Yes," she said.

His hand moved back to her breast. He rubbed his thumb over her hard nipple. The sensation was delicious. "This?" he asked as his lips brushed hers. "Do you want this?"

Gooseflesh covered Everly's skin, yet she wanted a more intimate touch. "Yes," she gasped.

Wyatt's fingers trailed from her chest to her waist. He opened a button on her pants and pulled down the zipper, exposing the lace at the top of her panties. His hand slipped inside the fabric. She was already wet. He applied the slightest pressure to the top of her sex, rubbing in a slow circle.

"Do you want me to do this?" he asked.

"I want *you*, Wyatt," she said.

Already, Everly could feel that she was being taken away by the current of yearning. In answer to his question, she rocked her hips forward and opened her thighs, offering herself to Wyatt. He buried his finger inside of her and her muscles clenched around him. He began to use long, slow strokes. She reached for Wyatt, pulling his mouth to hers. She kissed him deeply, hungrily, as if she might never be sated.

He pulled away from the kiss. His thumb stroked the top of her sex and his fingers still moved inside of her. "Look at me," he said.

Slowly, she met his gaze.

"You are so beautiful, Everly Baker. I want to watch you. Your eyes. Your mouth. The flush of your cheeks. I want you to see me."

He thrust inside her again, harder this time. Everly gasped. Her skin was too close-fitting, and she feared that she might burst with unfulfilled longing. Wyatt continued to bring her pleasure with his hand and her eyes never left his. His jaw tensed, and his dark gaze held yearning, barely restrained. Yet, there was more to his look. He saw Everly—truly saw her. He saw her loss and fear and determination. He understood her need for more than justice, but vengeance.

And he didn't find her lacking for the flaws.

A haze filled her vision as Wyatt brought her closer to the brink of passion. She tried to focus on him, his deep brown eyes, the stubble on his chin. It was no use. She was too close to the edge. Her eyelids fluttered closed. Resting her head back on the cold glass, Everly cried out as she finally let go.

Wyatt's mouth was on hers, smothering her cries of delight with his hot kisses.

"I'm not done with you," he said. "Not by a long shot."

The echoes of her pleasure still resonated through her body, and her knees were weak. "You aren't done with me," she teased lightly. "My legs won't even hold me upright."

"No need," said Wyatt, as he held himself above her. An amber glow from the fire shone from behind, casting him in shadow. Nothing seemed real and yet, this was no dream.

Wyatt slipped off one of Everly's boots. He pressed his strong fingers into the pad of her foot, easing away tension she never knew she held.

"That feels good," she purred.

"You like?" he asked.

She bit her bottom lip and nodded.

He removed her other boot. He massaged the second foot, his eyes never leaving hers. He tugged on her pants and she lifted her hips. He slid off her slacks and dropped them in a heap. Sitting up, she pulled off her sweater, adding it to the pile. She shivered, despite the fire that blazed in the hearth.

"You can't be cold."

"Lace and satin don't keep in much heat," she said, referring to her bra and panties.

"Let's see what we can do about warming you up," said Wyatt. He backed off the window seat and kneeled on the floor. "Open your knees for me."

She did as he ordered. He moved to her, lifting her thighs over his shoulders. He pulled aside the stride of her underwear and placed his mouth on her sex.

Everly bucked against him. The pleasure was so intense that she wanted to run, escape to a place where she was in control.

Wyatt pleasured Everly with his mouth and his hands. Caressing. Tasting. Exploring. Worshipping. The ecstasy was too much. She climaxed for a second time, crying out his name.

"Still not done," said Wyatt.

He stripped out of his shirt and jeans. He was hard, as she knew he would be. But it was more than that—he was truly a work of art. His pecs were chiseled, his stomach was flat. A dark sprinkling of hair covered his chest and narrowed to a strip that dove to his groin. He stood and turned, giving her a full view of his tight rear and long legs.

While she was admiring Wyatt Thornton in all his male power, he'd taken a moment to retrieve a condom from his wallet. Everly was happy that he was prepared to be safe for both of them.

"Can I help with that?" she asked.

He handed her the foil packet. "Sure," he said.

Everly removed the condom and unrolled it down his length.

He moved to her, his lips on hers. She held tight to his shoulders as he spread her open, and then he was inside her. She wrapped her legs around his waist, taking him in deeper, needing him more.

She ran her hands through his hair. Down his back. She cupped his buttocks as they tightened and flexed with each thrust. She felt his strong arms and broad shoulders. His skin was hot and dampened with sweat. He was all muscle and sinew. Solid. Powerful. Unbreakable. His strokes increased. Faster. Harder. Wyatt threw back his head and gave a guttural howl.

He kissed Everly deeply, pressing his chest into hers. Their hearts shared a rhythm. The sky had turned from violet to indigo and the Rocky Mountains were now lost in the darkness.

Leaving a kiss on her shoulder, Wyatt rolled off Everly and strode to the half bath, closing the door behind him.

Taking advantage of the moment, Everly donned her panties and sweater. When Wyatt returned, she was sitting on the sofa, with a table lamp aglow.

"Hey, there," he said as he approached. He was still gloriously naked.

"Hey there, yourself," she said back.

"About what just happened…" He scratched the back of his head, lengthening the muscles of his torso and arms. "We should talk."

Everly wasn't in the mood to parse through feelings, not when her toes still tingled with pleasure. "We had mind-blowing sex," she said.

Wyatt pulled on his pants. "Mind-blowing, eh?"

"Yeah," she said. "Mind-blowing."

He chuckled and sat down beside her. She tried not to gawk at his bare chest, to recall the feel of his hard muscles. It was a wasted effort. Even though Everly didn't want to chat about their escapades—or any ensuing feelings—the silence left her fidgety.

"It's so quiet out here," she said, blurting out the first lame thing that came to mind.

He harrumphed and slipped a T-shirt over his head.

Everly should take the clue and keep her mouth shut but was compelled to fill the silence with something— anything. "Doesn't it bother you?"

Wyatt shrugged. "At first, sure. Las Vegas is a noisy place, and everyone gets used to their environment. It's the same with the quiet and slower pace."

"Do you ever miss it?" she asked. "Having a job, working, being social."

"Who says I'm not social?"

"I kind of figured it out," she teased. "But you're still hiding. Will you ever come out?"

Wyatt leaned back on the sofa and pinched the bridge of his nose. "Do I miss the real world?" he asked. "Honestly, sometimes."

"Let's say that Larry is the killer and you catch him," said Everly. "What would you do? Would you stay here, or would you go back to work for the FBI?"

"You're assuming a lot. First, that Larry's the killer and second, that the Bureau wants me back."

Everly tucked her legs beneath her. "Humor me."

"Maybe," he said. "Assuming that everything you said was true. Larry's the killer. I build a case. The FBI wants me. I might go back."

A little thrill of excitement ran up Everly's spine. Would Wyatt want to go to Chicago? They would make a fabulous couple... But she quickly pushed the notion from her mind. Really, it was ridiculous to even consider and yet, she could hardly think of anything else.

Before Everly could say anything, Wyatt's cell phone buzzed from where he'd left it on the desk. Everly's heart stilled, and she was taken back to the moment when she got the call—the one from Sheriff Haak, telling her that Axl was dead.

Her pulse began again as Wyatt crossed the room. He lifted the phone from the desk and glanced at the screen. "It's Davis, my contact with the LVPD," he announced before answering the call. "Hello?" he said, and then after a beat, added, "Let me put you on speaker so I can write all this down."

Everly rose to her feet as Wyatt sat at the desk and pulled a pad and paper from a drawer. "Go ahead," he said.

Davis cleared his throat. "I've got an employment history for Lawrence Walker." Davis then listed the names of three different casinos and a corresponding set of dates. Larry hadn't held any one job for longer than a few months. "I only have his name on a single lease. He lived in the same apartment for nineteen months. Grand Canyon Gardens. Small. Inexpensive. Not too far from the Strip."

As far as Everly could tell, they were getting information but nothing useful.

"Any roommates?" Wyatt asked.

"The lease doesn't say, but he had a two-bedroom unit."

Wyatt scribbled some notes, then said, "Thanks for the information. Anything else?"

"I was thinking about taking a ride by the Grand Canyon Gardens on my way home, see if any neighbors remember anything helpful," said Davis.

"Let me know what you find out, will you?"

"If it finally helps catch that monster, I'm willing to do anything." Then Davis ended the call.

"What do we do now?" Everly asked, suddenly aware of the fact that she was only in her top and panties.

"I'm going to cross-reference the victims in Las Vegas to Larry's employment history and see if anyone was a guest at a hotel where he worked."

Everly scooped up her discarded clothing from the floor. "I'll get dressed and be right back to help you," she said.

Wyatt had already powered up his computer and had the case's flash drive in hand. He turned in his seat and pinned her with his dark eyes. "If Larry's the killer, we'll prove it."

Everly nodded and slipped into the half bath. She dressed and turned on the tap. Holding her hands under the running water, she let it sluice through her fingers. She needed to find Axl's killer, but what if it wasn't Larry? Or worse, what if it was but they couldn't prove it?

It was obvious that Wyatt had his doubts about Larry Walker's guilt. Now that same worry gnawed at her middle. What if Wyatt was right and Larry wasn't involved at all? Still, Everly wouldn't accomplish anything by hiding in the bathroom. She splashed water on her face and turned off the tap.

Somewhat refreshed, Everly dried her face and opened the door.

Wyatt sat in front of the computer. After running a hand through his hair, he cursed.

"What is it?" Everly asked.

"None of the victims stayed at a hotel where Larry worked." He pressed the heels of hands into his eyes. With a mirthless laugh, he said. "It was really stupid to think that we'd bumble around and find a killer who's eluded law enforcement for years."

"There has to be more," said Everly. Her pulse raced and the metallic taste of fear and desperation filled her mouth. "I went to Reno a few years back for work. It's not Vegas, but the setup is similar. You stay at one hotel, but you might gamble at another, eat at the next and see a show at a fourth."

Wyatt waved his hand at the screen. "See for yourself. I have credit-card receipts for all activities. None of them are at the hotels where Larry worked."

"He might have gone to a different casino," Everly offered. "And if he paid with cash, there wouldn't be a credit-card record."

"He might have, but we need proof—not guesses."

Everly's cheek stung as if she'd been slapped. Biting her bottom lip, she counted to ten. It wouldn't do to say exactly what she was thinking. Instead, she pulled up a chair and sat next to Wyatt. "Let's start from the beginning. What do we know about the first victim?"

Wyatt moved the mouse and opened up a file. It was all there—the victim's name, age, occupation.

Hometown. Reason for his visit. Everly read the information again and again. Nothing. She pointed to the last line—reason for visit. "It says that the victim was in Las Vegas for a family wedding."

"So? Lots of people get married in Las Vegas."

"That's true, but was it a destination wedding, where everyone traveled to the ceremony? Or did the wedding take place in Las Vegas because that's where the bride and groom lived?"

Wyatt sat back in the chair and cupped his chin in his hand. "I think it was a cousin who got married. She was a graduate student at UNLV."

"Do you have her address?"

Wyatt jiggled the mouse. "I do."

He opened another document. Everly leaned forward, every muscle tense.

They both silently scanned the page. Wyatt pointed to a line in the text. "She lived in graduate-student housing," he said. "But it was a good thought."

Everly tried to tell herself that there was much more information to sift through. Yet, she'd been so sure. "What about the fiancé?" she asked.

"I get that you're disappointed," said Wyatt. "There are some connections, but we need something a little more substantial than Larry living in both places at the time of the killings."

Everly wasn't ready to give up. "It seems like a lot to me," she said.

"It's mostly circumstantial," he said.

"So that's it? You're quitting?"

"You have to understand, sometimes you follow a set of clues and they lead nowhere."

"What do we do now?"

Wyatt shook his head. "There is nothing more to do."

Rising to her feet, Everly paced around the room. "You're afraid of making another mistake." She paused. "I saw the OPR's report."

The minute she spoke, Everly knew she'd made a mistake.

Wyatt's eyes flashed with rage and for the first time, she understood that he might be as dangerous as the killers he hunted. When he spoke, his words were measured but his voice was filled with steel. "You had no right to go pawing through my things…"

"Paw through your things?" she asked, interrupting. "The report was in the file *you* handed to me." Working her jaw back and forth, Everly continued, "You arrested a man, but knew he was innocent. Why would you hide the alibi?"

"That's not what happened," he said.

"Oh really? Illuminate me with the truth."

"Nah," he said with the shake of his head. "It's not worth it."

Everly wanted to leave—to get away from him. But where would she go? Glancing over her shoulder, she looked at Wyatt. He was typing on the computer, oblivious to her, or her anger.

She started to walk away.

"Wait," he said. "You need to see this."

"What is it?"

Wyatt didn't bother looking her way. "I found a concrete link that connects Larry Walker to the first victim."

Everly went numb. "What is it?"

"Neither the bride nor the groom lived at Canyon Gardens Apartments," said Wyatt. "But a member of the wedding party did."

"Is that enough to arrest Walker?" Everly asked, her heart racing.

He shook his head. "Arresting him is up to the sheriff," said Wyatt. "But it's enough to bring Larry in for a serious conversation."

Chapter 10

Wyatt itched with the need to act, yet he knew that a certain amount of preparation was necessary if they were going to track Larry Walker down and speak to him. There was more that he knew—and hadn't been willing to say before. Now, Wyatt knew what Larry had been hiding. Yet, before speaking to the cook, he wanted to make two calls. The first was to Sheriff Haak.

He finally reached the sheriff at home. When Haak answered on the fifth ring, Wyatt activated the phone's speaker feature. Haak's voice was thick with sleep. "This better be good," he said.

Wyatt glanced at the clock on his computer screen—11:00 p.m. already? Not that the time mattered. "This is Wyatt Thornton. You needed a connection between Larry Walker and the victims from Las Vegas," said Wyatt. "And I have one."

The sheriff took in a quick breath. "I'm awake."

"The first victim was in Las Vegas for a cousin's wedding. The bride—his cousin—was a student at UNLV and she lived on campus."

"You woke me up for that?"

Wyatt bit back a curse and continued. "It's not the cousin, but one of the people in the wedding party. He and Larry Walker lived in the same apartment complex."

The line went silent. Everly stood near Wyatt. He did his best to not look in her direction. After the words exchanged about the OPR's report…well, Wyatt wasn't sure what he thought about her now.

If he was honest with himself, he was more concerned about what she thought of him.

"You sure about that?" Haak asked.

The question drew Wyatt from his reverie. "Positive," he said. "Do you know where Larry is now?"

"Give me a minute," the sheriff said. "I'll call the deputy I assigned to watch Larry from my cell phone."

The sound of voices was unmistakable in the background. Too bad Wyatt couldn't make out a word of what was being said.

"You there?" Sheriff Haak asked.

As if Wyatt would hang up. "I'm here."

"My deputy says that Larry's still at the Pleasant Pines Inn."

"Is the pub crowded tonight?" Wyatt needed all

the information he could get in order for a successful apprehension.

"Closed," said the sheriff.

"Closed? It's only eleven o'clock. That's kind of early, isn't it?" Everly asked.

The sheriff said, "Sometimes they shut down if there isn't much of a crowd."

"But Larry's still there," said Wyatt. He hated that their prime suspect hadn't been placed into custody. Yet, it was the sheriff's call who got arrested and when. Then again, maybe the Sheriff Haak was smarter than Wyatt. Hadn't it been a mishandled arrest that cost Wyatt his career?

"He hasn't been seen leaving the building and his truck is in the lot," said the sheriff. "The deputy thinks that he's having an after-work drink by himself."

The late-night cocktail followed what they knew of Larry's behavior. Yet, it wasn't the absolute answer Wyatt wanted. Still, it was the best they were going to get. "We're on our way, Sheriff."

"I figured as much," said Haak. "I'll meet you there."

Wyatt ended the call and entered another number.

"This is Marcus Jones."

"Marcus," said Wyatt. "We have a connection between Larry and one of the victims. Larry's still at the pub." He hesitated. "Feel like a beer?"

"I thought you'd never ask."

As promised by Sheriff Haak, Larry's truck was in the employee parking lot of the Pleasant Pines Inn.

A single light was attached to the back wall and illuminated the rear door.

The plan was straight forward. Marcus Jones and Sheriff Haak would go in to the hotel through the lobby. The sheriff had jurisdiction, since the supposed crimes had occurred in his county. He'd be the one to arrest Walker. Marcus Jones was with the sheriff for added reinforcement, if needed.

Wyatt was to come in from the back and go directly to the pub. The deputy, Travis Cooper, was to remain in the parking lot, covering the rear egress and Larry's truck—the most likely means of escape.

Wyatt was ready. It was moments like this where Wyatt felt as he truly understood what it was to be alive—to have a purpose.

With his SIG Saur tucked into his waistband at the small of his back he turned to Everly. "I want you to stay in my truck. If anything happens, leave."

"And go where?" she asked, her tone as cold and hard as the metal of the firearm tucked into the small of his back.

"Go to the RMJ offices," he said. Belatedly, he realized that he should have left Everly there in the first place. It was too late now to correct his mistake and he continued, "That'll be the safest place for you."

"How many times do I have to tell you that I'm not worried about my own safety? I only care about catching my brother's murderer."

Wyatt was desperate to catch the killer, as well. It's just that he cared far more about keeping Everly from harm's way than anything else. The thought struck him like a fist to the chin. Sure, they'd become lovers, but Wyatt didn't love Everly, right?

"I'd argue with you," he said to Everly, "but it won't help. I know it."

"No," she said. "It won't."

"You can come, but you have to do exactly as I say. One wrong move and you could get shot."

"I understand," said Everly.

Wyatt used a crowbar, provided by the sheriff's office, and pried the door open. It led to the same hallway he'd chased Larry down that morning. His pulse raced like he was still running, his breath echoed in his ears. He drew his gun and stepped lightly, listening for sounds beyond those of his footfalls on the floor. Ahead was the pocket door to the conference room where they'd held the meeting. The hallway continued, ending at the back of the main pub, where they'd hopefully find an unsuspecting Larry.

Wyatt held Everly's hand as he pushed open the door. It gave a whisper of sound.

"Stay with me," he whispered to Everly.

She gripped his hand tighter. "I'm not going anywhere."

A recessed light illuminated a long, mahogany bar. A mirror hung on the wall and showed a reflection of the room. Tables, with chairs placed on top. An empty dance floor, with parquet tiles. A forgotten mop and bucket. No Larry.

Marcus Jones and Sheriff Haak came through the doors adjacent to the lobby.

"Anything?" Marcus asked.

"Nada," said Wyatt.

"Which means he's somewhere," said Everly.

"Unless he snuck away," said Wyatt. "And left his truck as a decoy."

All eyes turned to the sheriff. If Larry had escaped, his office would be to blame. "I'll see if the front desk has video of the last two hours," said Haak.

"I'll do a floor-by-floor search," said Marcus.

"Everly and I will check through the kitchen and restaurant."

With a nod, Marcus and the sheriff left to do their tasks. Another door was tucked into the back corner.

"That's got to be the kitchen," said Everly.

"Stay behind me," said Wyatt. He pulled his weapon again as he slowly pushed open the door. The room was black as pitch. A faint light from the pub seeped in and spread across the threshold. There was a faint creaking. The room stank of ammonia… and blood. Wyatt immediately recognized the stench. He ran his hand along the wall, searching for a light switch. Using the flat of his hand, he flipped all the switches upward.

The room filled with blinding light.

A piercing scream filled the small kitchen, and the noise ricocheted off the steel appliances. Wyatt spun to the sound. Everly stood on the threshold, her face chalky white. She lifted a trembling hand and pointed to an alcove at the back of the room.

Hanging from a noose was the body of Larry Walker.

* * *

Larry hung by his neck, the rope slowly swinging. His complexion was gray, and a trickle of blood leaked from his mouth. His eyes were open, even in death. A chair was lying on the ground, toppled to the side, from where he'd kicked it away.

Everly began to shiver. Wyatt was at her side. He placed a hand on her shoulder.

"It's okay," he said.

"No," she said, her voice shrill. "It's not."

"Don't look. Look at me," Wyatt insisted.

She moved her gaze to his face. His dark brown gaze anchored her. Slowly, she stopped shivering.

"Wyatt! Everly!" Sheriff Haak stood on the threshold, breathing heavily. "I heard screaming." His color faded as he took in the scene. With a gasp, he asked, "Dear God, what happened?"

"It's a suicide," said Everly, surprised that she'd found her voice and even happier to use it. "Larry knew that we suspected him of all the murders. Then he killed himself before being caught."

"It doesn't make sense," said Wyatt. "Serial killers typically don't commit suicide."

"There's a piece of paper on that table," said the sheriff. He pointed to the stainless steel workspace in the middle of the room. He ambled over to investigate.

Placing his palms on either side of the page, he began to read out loud. "'I'm not going to apologize for what I've done. Those men deserved to die—every last one of them. I'm not going to tell you why

I did what I did. You wouldn't understand. I'm tired of hiding and running and being afraid of getting caught. Today was the closest I've ever come to being apprehended and I'm not going to jail.'

"It's not addressed to anyone in particular," said Sheriff Haak.

Everly remained mute, but she suspected that Larry had written the note for Wyatt's sake.

The sheriff continued, "Nor is it signed."

"How can we tell if the note really came from Larry?" Everly asked.

"Who else would write this?" the sheriff asked.

He had a point. Everly shrugged.

"It'll be easy to prove whether it is his or not. All we need is a confirmed writing sample from Larry Walker and a handwriting expert," said Wyatt. He continued, "Even if Larry wrote this note, I still don't like this. Serial killers aren't afraid. They don't feel remorse. None of this is typical."

Pulling the phone from his pocket, Wyatt placed a call. "Marcus," he said. "Come into the kitchen, we found Larry." He paused, listening to the answer, and hung up.

"I need to call Doc Lambert and have him collect the body," said the sheriff. He exited the kitchen, leaving Everly and Wyatt alone.

"If you want to go and wait in the pub," he said, "you can."

The offer was tempting. In fact, Everly wanted to get away from Larry's unrelenting stare. Yet, this man had taken her brother's life. She owed it to Axl to see the investigation through to the end. She shook her head. "I'll stay," she said.

"Suit yourself," said Wyatt. He approached the body.

"What are you doing?" Everly asked, her pulse racing. "This is a crime scene. You can't tamper with evidence."

"Technically," said Wyatt. He spotted a box of plastic gloves on one of the counters, used for food prep, grabbed a pair and slipped them on, then patted down the corpse. "It hasn't officially been labeled a crime scene yet, although you are right about the evidence tampering."

She cast a quick glance over her shoulder. "Then what are you doing?"

"Looking for something to connect Larry to the killings."

Using two fingers, Wyatt withdrew a wallet from Larry's back pocket. He brought the wallet to the island and set it down. It was nylon with Velcro closures. Wyatt opened the main compartment. There was fifty dollars in cash and a driver's license, along with two credit cards. Inside was another compartment, hidden behind the first. The material bulged.

"There's definitely something in here," said Wyatt as he opened the second section.

Everly moved closer to get a better view. Larry had hidden away dozens of bills. "More money?" she asked.

Wyatt pulled them out. "Not just money. He has a stack of two-dollar bills—all of them have been ripped in half. My guess, each of these bills matches the other halves found on each of the victims."

Carl Haak hated that his department was so small they needed Rocky Mountain Justice—an organization new to Pleasant Pines and he knew next to nothing about—to process the scene, taking photos, dusting for fingerprints, collecting evidence. He hated that his deputy, Travis Cooper, was looking to Marcus Jones for leadership. He hated that, even though there were only three RMJ operatives—Julia McCloud, Luis Martinez, and Marcus Jones, the trio were top-notch at their jobs. But what he hated the most was that Larry Walker never should've gotten away with so many killings in Pleasant Pines, and that responsibility belonged to Carl.

He'd failed the town in more ways than he cared to count. With his retirement in a couple weeks, he'd never make amends. His gut was filled with painful acid. He'd called in Dr. Lambert to collect the body. With the spate of serial killings, Doc Lambert didn't want to be too hasty this time around and he refused to name a cause of death or call it a suicide. All the same, it seemed obvious to Carl Haak—Larry Walker knew he was about to get arrested. To avoid spending the rest of his life in jail, he had taken his own life.

At the scene, Carl had catalogued the stack of two-dollar bills, torn in half, found in Larry's wallet. The way Carl saw it, Larry had placed one half of a bill with each victim and then he'd kept the other for himself—a macabre souvenir from a kill. Since more than twenty bills—all ripped in half—had been found, it meant that Larry had taken more lives than anyone had ever guessed.

It also meant that people other than Carl had missed the obvious. Still, it was the most singularly humiliating moment in his long life.

"Sheriff?" someone asked. It was one of the guys from RMJ—Martinez. He was an ex-cop from Denver, and even though he was thirty years Haak's junior, he knew his way around the scene better than the sheriff ever would. "Did you want to organize a team to search Larry's home?"

That was another thing that grated on Carl's nerves—all these impressive operatives running a search while trying to make Carl, the failure, feel like he was in charge.

After a moment's pause, he said, "Why don't you do it?"

The big guy held a camera that cost more than Carl's monthly mortgage payment and looked over his shoulder. It was obvious that he was taking pictures for evidence and didn't want to leave before the task was done.

"I'll do it," Wyatt Thornton offered. "I want to get into that bastard's house and see what else he has from previous victims. You should probably come with me, Sheriff."

It was a measly bone thrown to an old dog.

"Yeah," said Carl as he pushed himself to stand.

His knees creaked with the effort. "Sure. Travis," he called to the deputy.

The young man was working with the female operative, Julia, a tall blonde with her long hair pulled into a ponytail.

Travis said, "Yeah, Sheriff?"

"You stay here and..." He paused, not sure what to say. "I'm going to Walker's house and see what's what."

Wyatt turned to Everly Baker. "I'm going with the sheriff to look at Larry Walker's house. You should stay here. Maybe get a room and try to rest."

"No way," said Everly. "I still haven't found my brother's camera. What if Larry had it?"

"You can come along if you want," Wyatt offered.

Everly accepted a little too quickly for it to only be about her brother's camera—something that could be brought to her if found.

Carl studied Wyatt and Everly as they walked from the pub and into the lobby.

Despite her tenacity, Sheriff Haak had come to like Everly. If it hadn't been for her urging, nobody would have ever looked into her brother's death, or any of the others. He hoped that once she went home, she'd rebuild her life and maybe find peace.

They headed through the lobby. The front door opened and Darcy Owens, the desk clerk, stepped in from the night. Her blond hair fell loose around her shoulders. Wrapped up in a heavy coat, she wore sweatpants and sneakers.

"Is it true, Sheriff?" she asked in a breathless whisper. "The owner called me and said that Larry committed suicide." Her voice cracked on the last word.

"He did." Carl hitched his pants by the belt loops. "Hanged himself in the kitchen."

Darcy went pale. "Why?"

Wyatt stepped forward and answered her question with one of his own. "How well did you know Larry?"

Darcy appeared to be taken aback by Wyatt's question. "How well do I know him?" she said. "Well enough, I guess."

"Did you socialize with Larry?"

"Occasionally, the employees would have drinks in the pub after it closed. The inn holds parties for employees a couple of times a year. I've hosted game night at my house. Larry was always invited." She chewed on her bottom lip. "What's all of this about?"

"It seems that none of us knew Larry as well as we thought we did," said Carl.

Twin dots of red appeared on Darcy's cheeks. "What's all this about?" she asked again. This time there was an edge to her question.

Carl shifted from one foot to the next. He wasn't ready to tell folks what was happening; or admit that he'd failed at his singular task of keeping the town safe.

"It seems as if your tip paid off," Wyatt said for him. "Larry was involved in Axl Baker's death."

Darcy's jaw dropped.

Everly stepped forward. "I'm going to miss my

brother every day for the rest of my life. Now I know what happened—or, at least who was to blame."

Darcy wiped tears from her eyes. "I'm just so sorry."

"It's not your fault," said Everly. "Besides, if you hadn't pointed us in Larry's direction, we never would've figured any of this out."

"Wyatt," Darcy breathed. "You caught the killer."

Yep, Carl had been right about Wyatt Thornton from the get-go. The man had the kind of looks that made the ladies go gaga. "Well, Darcy, if you think of anything, you let me know," said Carl.

"There is one thing," said Darcy. "One night, when we were all having an after-hours drink, Larry became really sad. Like, really, really sad. I asked him what was wrong, and, he told me that he'd... done things in Vegas."

Carl's shoulder blades pinched together. "What kind of things?"

Darcy chewed on her lip.

"You have to tell us," said Wyatt. "Larry's gone and you don't need to protect him anymore."

"And besides," added Everly, "there are other family members, like me, who want to know what happened to their loved ones."

"I'm not sure that it's much. I mean, at first, he told me that he'd had legal troubles with some girlfriends. Fights that got out of hand, that kind of thing."

"And then?" Everly persisted, when Darcy didn't seem to know what to say.

"Well, I told him that we all have issues and exes who've treated us badly. He said it was more than that. He told me that he thought he was evil."

A chill ran down Carl's spine. "He actually told you that?"

"At the time, I thought that it was the whiskey and he was just depressed. But it seems like he might've been right. If Larry did kill Axl Baker, and those other men, then maybe he was right. Maybe Larry really was evil."

"You might have to talk to Chloe Ryder," said the sheriff. "She's the new district attorney."

"Chloe Ryder," Darcy repeated. "There was a social work intern at my high school named Chloe Ryder. I wonder if it's the same person."

Before Haak could respond, Marcus Jones approached at a trot. "I was examining the body and I think there's something you need to see." He held a fancy camera, with an illuminated screen.

"Can you give us a moment," the sheriff said to Darcy.

"Sure thing," she replied, before heading over to the reception desk.

Marcus paused for a moment, no doubt waiting for Darcy to be out of earshot, before holding up the camera. Everly and Wyatt moved in close.

"See this," Marcus said, showing a picture of hands, mottled and purple.

Carl said, "I see the fingers of a dead person, but I assume there's more."

Marcus made the picture bigger. "Look here. The fingertips are scratched."

Sure enough, the pads of the thumb and two fingers were scraped raw. "Do you think he struggled? And was forcibly hanged?" Carl wasn't going to miss any obvious signs of foul play a second time.

"I think we need to consider every angle," said Marcus.

"Or his hands might've gotten scraped when I tackled him in the parking lot," said Wyatt. "Or he might've struggled during strangulation. Even if Larry was determined to kill himself, his instinct would've been to claw at the rope."

"And he worked in the kitchen," added Everly. "As a cook I imagine that he was always getting burned or cut."

For Carl, the simplest explanations were usually true. But that belief had caused a heap of grief and he wasn't about to make the same mistake again.

Chapter 11

Larry Walker had lived in a small apartment at the back of a run-down house. It consisted of a kitchen/living room combination, a single bedroom in the rear and small bathroom between the two. From the Spartan furnishings to the lack of acquired junk, it was obvious that Larry didn't have much use for material possessions.

"How long has Larry been in Pleasant Pines?" Everly asked. "Two years? Three? Doesn't it seem odd that he has next to nothing?"

There were other things about Larry's apartment that bothered Wyatt more. "Here's what gets me the most," said Wyatt. "There's absolutely nothing to connect Larry to any of the killings—not even Axl's missing camera." He continued, "You saw that stack of money. If each bill represents a killing, then Larry is responsible for over twenty murders. Keeping personal belongings from the victims illustrates the power of the killer. In short, I'd expect to see trophies from each of the victims—and we haven't found any yet."

"Or maybe that's just it," said Everly. "Larry hasn't been a typical serial killer, if there is such a thing, from the beginning. Maybe that's why he'd gotten away with his crimes for so long."

Maybe Everly was right. Could Larry be a new breed of serial killer? One that could seamlessly blend in to society? Or had Larry just gotten lucky, been smart enough to kill without arousing suspicion? Even that idea was hardly satisfactory. It brought back the original question. "Then where is the camera? We already know from the initial discovery of your brother that it's not near the old schoolhouse."

"Easy," said the sheriff. "Wyoming is a big state. Larry could've dumped it almost anywhere."

Wyatt knew, deep in his bones, that Larry hadn't committed suicide. Like a magician's sleight of hand, all eyes had been directed to what the real killer wanted them to see—leaving the actual crimes hidden.

The real question was, what next?

"There's not much more we can do here tonight," he said. Wyatt glanced at his phone for the time— 3:15 a.m. "This morning," he corrected.

"You folks go on ahead," said the sheriff. "I'm

going to close off the crime-scene, then head back to the inn and see how everything is progressing. I need to check in with Deputy Cooper and send him home. I imagine that we can release your brother's body in the morning, Everly. Then you can take him home and give him a proper burial."

Everly gave a wan smile. "Thanks for everything, Sheriff," she said.

"Don't thank me," he said. "If it wasn't for you, we never would've looked into any of these deaths. Without you, Larry would've kept getting away with murder." Hooking his fingers through his belt loops, the sheriff hefted up his pants. "I reckon that it's me who should be thanking you."

She flashed him a grateful smile, then turned to the door.

"One last thing," said the sheriff. "Don't talk to the media right away. I need to contact the next of kin for all the other victims. That'll take some time. Don't want them to hear it on the news."

Wyatt said, "You don't have to worry about me. I'm not exactly a big fan of reporters."

Sheriff Haak nodded. "I can't exactly blame you for that." The older man turned to Everly. "I hope you'll come and visit us now and again—when the circumstances of your stay are more pleasant."

"I'd like that, Sheriff," she said. She opened her arms. The sheriff leaned in for a hug and patted her back.

"Although, I'm retiring in a couple of weeks and

moving to South Carolina. You might need to come and visit me at the beach."

"It's a date," said Everly with a small wave. She walked to the door. Wyatt was right at her heels and used the remote starter to unlock the auto. Everly slid into the seat next to Wyatt's.

"You look tired," he said, getting behind the wheel of his truck. He reached across her and placed his gun into the glove box.

"Then I must look phenomenal, because I feel exhausted."

Wyatt chuckled and backed down the short drive. He wasn't in the mood for conversation. He had too many thoughts—feelings—to deconstruct and was thankful for the silence.

The sky unfurled above him, an inky swath of velvet. "Must be cloudy."

"How do you know?"

Damn. He'd spoken out loud without meaning to. Over the years, he'd gotten so comfortable with his own company he forgot what it was like to have someone around who listened.

"No stars," he said.

Everly leaned forward in her seat and looked to the sky. "That's too bad. We never see the stars in Chicago." She was quiet for a moment. "There's a certain appeal to seeing stars."

Wyatt worked his jaw back and forth. "I was ordered to lie," he said. He'd never spoken about his ordeal to anyone—and he wasn't completely sure why he was speaking now. Maybe it was the darkness or the quiet or maybe it was because Wyatt was telling his secret to Everly.

Continuing, Wyatt said, "My higher-ups wanted a suspect in custody. The blackjack dealer had been on our radar, but we knew he had an alibi for one of the killings. I was told to arrest him anyway. The guy was smart. He hired a lawyer. The lawyer brought his alibi to the press and then we had to let him go. The whole case fell apart and I was the one who took all the blame."

She placed her hand on his thigh. "Wyatt, I'm so sorry."

"I don't want your sympathy," he said. "I just wanted you to know the truth." He paused. "The truth about what I did."

"I don't know what to say," she said.

"There's nothing to say." Wyatt turned his attention back to the road and the night.

The earlier silence, which had been soothing, was replaced by a chasm that separated Wyatt from Everly. At the same time, the quiet was filled with a single question. Now that Everly had forced Wyatt out of his sanctuary, would he ever be able to live a solitary life?

Everly stared out the window of the truck, seeing nothing of the surroundings. Fragments of memory flashed in and out of her mind. Larry's body, dangling from a noose. A faceless form reflected in the mirror. The old schoolhouse surrounded by mist.

Wyatt's driveway came into view and he eased

off the paved road. In the distance, the ancient farmhouse rose out of the barren landscape. She exhaled, relaxing farther into the seat. They were home.

Everly's spine stiffened at the word: home. Without her brother, would she ever feel like she belonged in Chicago again? True, Axl's job always took him to the far corners of the earth, but he came back between gigs. And now? Well, Everly had her job and friends.

What she lacked in Chicago was a family, people who loved her most of all.

Wyatt parked his truck next to her rental car, and she turned to face him. "Why don't you come back with me?"

"What?"

"Come to Chicago. You've solved the unsolvable case. The FBI must have a field office downtown. If you don't want to go back to the Bureau, there are tons of other places that would hire you." Everly was in her element, her heart rate creeping upward with excitement. "I can handle your comeback. I have contacts with all the major networks and can craft a press release that'll have you on every cable news channel by dinnertime tonight."

"What?" he asked again.

She hadn't stuttered. Maybe she'd spoken too fast for him to fully appreciate her plan. "You're a hero, Wyatt, and it's time that the world knows."

"You want me to move to Chicago?"

"You have to admit, it checks a lot of boxes for you—for us, really."

"Gus would hate living in a city. He's used to being able to run around."

"There are dog parks," said Everly.

"It's about freedom to roam. You don't have that in Chicago, do you?"

"Well, no," she admitted.

Before she could say anything else, Wyatt turned off the ignition and opened his door. The interior light filled the cabin with its unnatural glare. "And speaking of Gus, I need to let him out before he makes a mess in the house."

Jumping down from the truck, Wyatt slammed the door shut. Everly was surrounded in darkness once more. Yet, she didn't need the light to be able to see what was happening. She and Wyatt were different people, with different wants and different lives. And those differences were too much for a compromise.

Everly opened her own door and hopped from the big truck to the ground. She exhaled, her breath instantly freezing into a cloud. Everly's arms ached. Her back was sore. Her legs throbbed. She was exhausted and wanted nothing more than to sleep and sleep and sleep.

Yet for one glorious moment, Everly had seen the possibility of a future with Wyatt. What she envisioned had been perfect. Like most dreams, it faded with the coming dawn.

Reaching her arms above her head, she stretched and rotated, easing away some of her physical discomfort. Tilting her head back, she caught a glimpse of the sky. There, just above the horizon, was a brilliant light. A star, which had been hidden by the clouds, emerged.

Wyatt had gone into the house and returned with Gus. The dog whipped his tail back and forth so hard it was nothing more than a cream-colored blur. Gus nudged Everly's leg and she scratched the scruff of his neck. "Hey, boy," she said.

"You're right," she said to Wyatt. "I can't expect your dog to adjust to living in a city."

Gus trotted off, as if to give them privacy.

"So where does that leave us?" Wyatt asked.

"I can visit," she said. "You can come to Chicago now and then."

"You want to try to make something work out between us long-distance?"

From the dubious tone of his voice, she knew that he didn't like the idea.

"I don't think that would work," she said.

Wyatt sighed. "You're probably right."

Everly looked back to the sky, to the star. It was as if her brother was watching. The notion gave Everly a sense of calm, and yet she couldn't help but wonder what would Axl, the free spirit, recommend?

She didn't need to think about it for long. Axl would tell Everly to embrace life, and not look back. Without adventure, he would say, she wasn't living— she was just existing.

Gus ambled back from the darkness and sat on his haunches, waiting.

"You're welcome to stay for now." Wyatt opened

the front door. "It's late and you don't want to fall asleep while driving back to town."

"Sure," she said. "And thanks."

Everly crossed the threshold and stepped into the house. The building had to be over one hundred and fifty years old, built when things were made to last. More than being able to see the stars, Everly appreciated the connection to the land and to history.

Behind her, Wyatt kicked the door closed, making the darkened room even darker. He moved, a shadow in the blackness, and her pulse began to pound in her skull. She didn't fear for her own safety, but Wyatt was dangerous, nonetheless. Without question, Everly's heart would certainly break as soon as she left him.

"Where do you want to sleep?" His voice came from the gloom, swirling around her, becoming the air that she breathed.

"Upstairs," she said, "in the bed." Everly stopped, taking only a moment more to think before she spoke. "With you."

"You don't have to do that," he said. He moved toward her, the shadow becoming flesh.

"I know," she said. "But I want you. If all we have left between us is tonight, I want to take this memory home with me. Make love to me, Wyatt."

Wyatt took her hand in his. He pressed it to his chest. Beneath her palm, his heartbeat was strong and steady. "I'll miss you once you're gone."

She stepped closer. "Shut up," she said, "and kiss me."

His lips were on hers. The kiss was hungry and

possessive. She wrapped her arms around his neck. Sensations washed over her, cleansing Everly of every thought beyond Wyatt and the embrace.

Her fingers grazed the back of his neck. His lips moved to the hollow of her throat and the fire of passion began to burn, warming Everly with desire. Wyatt's hands were at the small of her back, drawing her to him. He was already hard and the memory of being filled by Wyatt came on so strong that Everly moaned.

She needed him closer, needed the heat of his flesh warming her, needed to become one with Wyatt again. She loosened his belt and Wyatt gripped both her wrists in one hand.

"This time it isn't going to be a mad rush," he said.

She was drawn into his banter. "Oh, yeah?" she asked. "What do you plan to do, then?"

"Enjoy myself," he said. He pressed his lips to her ear. "I'm going to enjoy myself as I explore every inch of your body and make you come again and again and again." His whispered words blazed down her shoulder, and Everly shivered with anticipation.

Everly was much more accustomed to action than delay and she wanted to explore Wyatt everywhere and all at once. Yet, there was an unmistakable attraction to being touched by an unhurried hand.

He held the back of her head, tilting Everly so she could only look at Wyatt. In truth, she didn't want to see anything beyond his face. His gaze was filled with the same heat of longing she felt building, sweltering, within.

Her wrists were still in his grasp. He gently lifted her arms above her head. She was stretched out long, her breasts lifted.

"Don't move," he said as he stepped away. From the darkness, he studied her form. "You are so beautiful."

She felt beautiful. And desirable. And unrestrained.

"Kiss me," she said.

"Beautiful and pushy," he teased.

"You want someone meek and timid?"

"Never," he said. "But I told you to stand there."

"Is this all about power? Control? Are you only teasing me, Wyatt?"

"Would you mind if I was?" he asked.

She dropped her arms and reached for Wyatt's hand. "Come with me," she said, pulling him toward the stairs. "Game time is over."

Wyatt let Everly lead him up the stairs. He liked that she took the initiative, even though he wanted to slowly strip Everly out of every piece of clothing she wore. For him, taking his time wasn't simply about power, as she had suggested. Wyatt wanted the moment to last. Because there was one thing he knew— in the morning, all he would have were memories.

It was dark at the top of the stairs and he was blind with need. He reached for Everly and claimed her with his mouth. She let out a noise, a little mew of surprise, and he grew harder—if that was even possible.

Wyatt pulled Everly into the bedroom. He lifted her sweater over her head. Her bra was black, all lace and silk—a testament to Everly's wicked and sexy nature.

Pulling the front of her bra down, he exposed her breasts. Each nipple was a perfect bud. Wyatt bent his head and took one nipple into his mouth. She gave a little cry of delight. God, he was going to explode if she didn't stop. She clung to his shoulders, her nails biting through the fabric of his shirt and gouging his flesh. The pain didn't bother him. It was another sign that Everly was as lost in passion as he was, and it gave Wyatt a sense of power.

Everly had been right when she accused Wyatt of playing games. He didn't mind teasing her a little. Maybe he did want control. He applied pressure with his teeth. This time, she hissed and thrust her chest forward.

"Wyatt," she breathed. "I want you. Now."

"I'm taking my time," he said. He unhooked the back of her bra and let the straps slide from her shoulders. The bra fell to the floor.

She grabbed the hem of his shirt and tugged it over his head. She pressed her palm to his chest, burning his flesh with her touch. "I want to feel your skin next to mine. I want you inside of me."

Wyatt was no longer able to ignore the primal draw of Everly. But it was more than sex—even more than the mind-blowing sex from earlier. It was the fact that when they were together, Wyatt wanted to be a better man—the kind of man she deserved.

Was it really possible to fall for a person so quickly and so hard?

He lifted her from the ground and carried her to the bed. He removed her boots, taking a moment to rub the instep of each foot. Wyatt tugged on each leg of her pants. Everly lifted her nicely shaped rear from the bed as he finished removing her slacks.

And there she was. His goddess in a pair of black lace panties.

Wyatt wanted to bury himself so deep inside of her that he could taste it.

"What?" she asked, a small smile pulling up at the corner of one lip. "What are you thinking?"

It was his opportunity to say something suave. Instead, he told her the truth. "I want you, Everly Baker. It's a need. A hunger. A thirst."

She reached for his belt and unfastened the buckle. Wyatt took over from there and stripped in seconds. From a bedside drawer, he found a condom and rolled it down his shaft.

"I love looking at you in your sexy little panties; but those have to go."

Everly pulled them off slowly. Hip. Thighs. Calves. Feet. Then she let them slip from her fingertips to the floor. Like a lion of the Serengeti, Wyatt pounced on Everly, his quarry. He entered her in one hard thrust. Everly fitted him perfectly. Wyatt felt a tingling at the back of his neck, as if a warning from his brain told him that he might be overcome with passion too soon. He eased back his hips, until just the tip remained inside. He used languid, full strokes to set the rhythm.

Yet, he was always balanced on the precipice, ready to tumble into oblivion. He focused on the sweat that dampened his brow. He tried not to think about Everly's full breasts, which pressed into his chest. Yet he reached for her, rolling a taut nipple between his finger and thumb.

"Wyatt," she gasped, her hips lifting, bucking against him.

His control wavered, but he needed to make sure she was satisfied. He reached between their sweat-slicked bodies and found the top of Everly's sex. She was swollen with want and he applied pressure as he rotated this thumb. She moaned, and her inner muscles tightened around him. She was close to a climax, he knew it. Funny, it was only his second time with Everly and already, he could read her like a book.

He hooked one of her legs over his shoulder, diving in deeper. He loved the way her lips parted and how her eyelashes gently fluttered on her cheeks. Her breath came in short gasps as she called out his name. "Wyatt. Wyatt. Wyatt."

She placed her lips on his, the little whimpers becoming part of the kiss. His strokes were fast and hard, and Wyatt wasn't sure how much longer he could hold off. Then she cried out one last time and her grip on his shoulders loosened as her inner muscles contracted and released.

Wyatt couldn't contain himself any longer. With his pulse racing, he gave a low growl and let go. The bass of his heartbeat resonated throughout his body and Wyatt collapsed with Everly beneath him. She was soft and sweetly scented and perfect in every way.

He searched for the right words to let her know… But, let her know what? That he'd changed in the last day and half. Yes, that was exactly it. Somehow, he was a better man for having known her. Even though their paths crossed briefly, he would miss her once she was gone. But the words escaped him, so instead he whispered, "I'll be right back. Gotta take care of the condom."

In the dim bathroom, Wyatt cleaned up as quickly as he could. He didn't need a light to see that Everly was important. What was keeping him in Pleasant Pines? He loved his old farmhouse, but he'd never completely unpacked. He didn't have a job. Or friends. Or any other connection to the community.

He'd used Gus as his first excuse, but Gus was a good dog. He could adjust to living somewhere new. Maybe a change was just what Wyatt needed—and it made sense that Everly was the catalyst for his new beginning. Barefoot, he padded back to his bedroom. Everly was lying on her side, one arm tucked beneath her head. Her eyes were closed, and her breathing was deep. He reached for her shoulder, ready to give a slight shake and tell her that perhaps he could give Chicago a try.

Yet, after losing her brother, being attacked, helping him discover Larry's identity and then finding the killer dead, well, Wyatt knew she was exhausted.

He got in the bed beside her. Settling in, with her back nestled into his chest, Wyatt draped his arm around her waist. Everly stirred in her sleep, reaching for his hand.

There was something about lying next to Everly, with her in his arms and their hands joined. It was an emotion—not happiness, it wasn't anything as sentimental or simple as joy or even bliss. It was like the calm that followed a storm. Then, Wyatt knew. With Everly, he'd become content. In the morning, he'd tell her he wanted to talk about a future together.

Chapter 12

Wyatt quickly fell into a deep sleep. In a haze-filled dream, he stood before a closed door. Pushing it open, Wyatt found Larry's corpse hanging from the ceiling of an industrial kitchen. The body gently swayed, as if in a light breeze. The piss stain on Larry's jeans was still damp. The eyes were closed. The room was silent, save for the slow and steady creak of the rope as it rubbed against the rafters.

He approached the body. Reaching out, his fingers inched closer and closer to the dead man's mottled and swollen hand. Like a viper, the hand struck, closing Wyatt's wrist in an unbreakable grip. He tried to pull away, but the icy hand was too strong.

Wyatt looked at the corpse. The eyes that had been shut were now open. "It was all right there for you to find," admonished the corpse. "How could you have missed everything? Will you even bother to look now?"

Wyatt was frantic to escape death's grip. He twisted and pulled. Nothing. He pried one finger up and then another, until he finally burst free and stumbled, slamming into a set of metal shelves. Pots and pans rained down, before clattering to the floor. The clanging morphed into a ringing and Wyatt woke in his own bed. He pulled a shaking hand down his face and realized it was slick with cold sweat.

Everly was still in bed beside him. Her hands were tucked under her cheek and he stroked the side of her arm, wanting nothing more than to wake her with a kiss.

The ringing came again. But this was no dream. He cursed as he threw back the covers, letting in the cold.

Everly stirred in her sleep. Wyatt grabbed his pants off the floor and fished the phone from a pocket. He swiped the call open and stepped onto the landing at the top of the stairs.

"Hello?" He held the phone up with his shoulder as he put on his jeans.

"Wyatt, this is Davis. I'm sorry to be calling so early, but I turned up some information and I thought you'd want to know right away."

"Sure," said Wyatt. He descended the stairs and turned on a light over his desk. He pulled a pad of paper and a pen toward him. "Go ahead."

"I went to the apartment complex and there was a

long-time resident who remembered Larry. The man said that his cat disappeared not long after Larry moved in. He always suspected Larry of doing something to the cat—that's why he remembered the name and photo I showed him."

Wyatt said, "Is he sure that it didn't get hit by a car or wander off and become a coyote's dinner?"

"Even though he suspected Larry, he knew that something else might've happened to his cat. He got another kitty. One day he sees Larry trying to coax the cat from beneath a bush, and then that cat disappeared, too."

"Cruelty to animals is a hallmark of a serial killer's progression," Wyatt said.

"That's exactly what I thought. So, I went to the manager of the complex and asked if I could search the place."

Obviously, Davis had been given permission and found something interesting, otherwise he wouldn't be calling before dawn. The line had gone silent. Wyatt waited a beat. "You still there?"

"I work homicide in Las Vegas. I've seen stuff. Weird stuff. Stuff I can't unsee."

"I can well imagine," said Wyatt. And honestly, he could. He used to be a profiler for the FBI, after all. "What's got you so shaken?"

"There was a compartment hidden behind the wall. It was full of dead cats—there were a dozen of them, at least."

"Cats? Even boarded up, they'd stink while decomposing. Wouldn't someone notice the smell?"

"That's just it, they'd been mummified. As in full-blown Pharaohs-of-Egypt-in-the-Pyramids kind of mummified. But there was more. We found a trophy from each of the Las Vegas victims with the cats."

Davis kept talking, detailing all the items he'd found. Wyatt was hardly paying attention. He'd stopped breathing, and his pulse echoed in his ears. How many lives had Larry taken? And Wyatt, the supposed expert, had never suspected him of a thing.

"There's something I need to tell you," Wyatt said, interrupting Davis. "Larry Walker is dead. We went to arrest him, and he'd hanged himself. He left a note confessing to some killings, although he wasn't specific. More than the confession, he had half of several two-dollar bills in his wallet. Five of them match those found with the men who died in Pleasant Pines."

"Dead?" said Davis. "I hadn't seen anything on the news or heard about it from my superiors."

"The local sheriff wants to keep the whole case under wraps until he contacts all the families. I imagine that the feds will get involved eventually and take over the case."

"Then have whoever ends up in charge call me. I still don't have an ID on Larry Walker's roommate."

Most serial killers were loners, needing privacy to carry out their murderous activities. That fact struck Wyatt as more than a little odd. Then again, it was another peculiarity to add to a long list of things that didn't make sense.

"He had a roommate?" Wyatt scribbled the word on the pad of paper and circled it several times.

"He did," Davis said. "He lived with a female."

"Are you sure?"

"The neighbor with the cat remembers a woman living with Larry."

"What about the complex manager?"

"She's new to the job, so Larry's time as a resident was before her arrival."

"What's your sense about the roommate? Was the woman an accomplice? A victim?"

"Your guess is as good as mine," said Davis.

"Can you do me two favors? First, don't mention what I told you about Larry being dead—or what we suspect about his serial killings."

"Suspect?" scoffed Davis. "I'd say the kitty tomb adorned with victims' trophies makes him a little more than a suspect."

Wyatt ignored the detective's comment and continued with his next request. "Second, get the neighbor to talk to a sketch artist. See if he can come up with a composite of the roommate."

"I'm one step ahead of you," said Davis. "The neighbor already talked to our artist, but they didn't come up with anything useful."

Wyatt cursed. "Even without the roommate's ID, you found a lot. Thanks again for everything. I owe you."

"I'll put it on your tab," said Davis before ending the call.

Wyatt set aside the phone and scrubbed his face

with his hands. His eyes burned from lack of sleep. His back ached from tackling Larry in the parking lot. For the first time, he noticed a scrape on his knuckles and another on his forearm.

A floorboard behind Wyatt creaked and he turned in his seat. Everly stood at the bottom of the stairs. She'd donned his discarded shirt. Her long legs were bare, and her hair cascaded around her shoulders and down her back.

"I woke up and you were gone," she said.

"Sorry about that. I got a call from Davis. He'd been to Larry's old apartment. He found a compartment hidden in the wall."

"That's odd," said Everly.

"It was full of mummified cats."

A horrified expression crossed her face. "I take that back. A concealed compartment full of dead pets is pretty twisted."

"And personal effects from the Las Vegas victims," Wyatt added.

"I know you had some reservations about Larry. Especially since he doesn't seem like a textbook serial killer. But doesn't the evidence seem to be pretty overwhelming?" she said.

Wyatt looked at the notes he'd scribbled. He recalled the cold fear that had awakened him from the dream about Larry. Something wasn't coming together.

He looked at Everly. "You're right. I mean, everything does seem to point to him as the doer. So why can't I shake the feeling that there's something more? Something that we've been missing all along?"

Everly watched Wyatt from across the room. He wore only a pair of pants and, even at a distance, she could see the cords of tension that ran from his shoulders to his neck. She longed to massage away whatever bothered him. But now, in the cold light of morning, this was a problem she had no idea how to solve.

"What's wrong?" she asked.

"There's more to this case," he said. "I can feel it."

"You keep saying that, but what other evidence could there be?" As she spoke, her pulse spiked, and her hands began to shake. "Someone with a criminal record or who is cruel to animals? Check. Evidence that connects Larry to the victims? Check. Or maybe you'd be happy with a confession? Got that, too. Sincerely Wyatt, I don't get you. You finally tracked down a notorious serial killer, why can't you be satisfied?"

Wyatt's eyes flashed with anger. He turned to the desk. The muscles in his back, neck and shoulders were tighter than before. "I'm plenty satisfied."

"You don't look it," she said.

"Just drop it, Everly. You might be good at manipulating the media, but you're hardly an expert on me."

"You think that's all I do? Influence news reports?"

"Am I wrong?"

"Completely," she said. "But this isn't about me—it's about you and your inability to let go of this case, even though it's over."

Wyatt got to his feet and began to pace. "What do you want me to say? That I lost everything because I couldn't find a serial killer? Now that he's been caught I should be able to snap my fingers and get back to normal? I've been messed up for so long that I don't remember what ordinary feels like."

"I don't believe that for a second," said Everly.

"Why not? Because you've fallen in love with the idea that you'll rehabilitate me and my career, and then we'll become some power couple in Chicago? Did it occur to you that is your dream and has nothing to do with me?"

He stopped pacing and turned to face her. "No serial killer has ever been caught because of dumb luck. This guy was methodical and careful. We just happened to stumble on our prime suspect, Larry. There was no 'solving—'" he made air quotes "—of this case. Everything that points us to Larry is circumstantial and convenient as hell."

Everly's throat burned with the need to scream. But she wouldn't allow herself to be goaded into a rage. She bit the inside of her lip until the moment passed. Inhaling deeply, she tried again. "I was the one who saw Axl's death as more than an accident. I forced you back into this case and you figured out what happened. What's so wrong with that?"

"Nobody forces me to do anything," he said.

A look flashed across his face, and then it was

gone. Had it been anger? Or was it hurt? What Everly wouldn't give to be a mind reader.

A whimpering came from the corner. Gus, his eyes downcast, stood near the front door. He lifted a paw and scratched at the jamb.

Everly dropped to the bottom step. She was exhausted by it all—her brother's death, the murder, the investigation. "I think your dog needs to go out," she said.

The sun was just starting to peek over the distant Rocky Mountains, turning the sky crimson and orange. Everly studied Wyatt from her perch on the steps. She wanted to go to him and fall into his muscled arms; to tell him she was sorry for being difficult. Yet, why?

Everly had stumbled into Wyatt's life. While she believed that luck had brought them together, in a few days, she'd realized that he was so much more than just a specialist to use for her own advantage.

He was smart, brave, careful, but still passionate. He was definitely not like any other man she'd ever met.

His toned chest rose and fell with each breath and she remembered the warmth of his flesh. The salty taste of his sweat. The musky scent of their shared passion.

Gus scratched the door a second time.

Wyatt said, "Let me get dressed, boy, and I'll take you for a walk."

He approached the stairs and held tight to the newel post. Their eyes met.

"I'll be gone for about fifteen minutes," he said. "Will you be here when I get back?"

Was that an invitation to stay? Or worse, a not-so-subtle suggestion to leave? In the end it didn't matter. Everly had come to Pleasant Pines with one goal—to discover what really happened to her brother, not to fall in love. She shook her head. "I think it's best if I get back to town. I don't know how complicated it is to transport a body, but I'm sure there are arrangements to be made."

"If you wait," said Wyatt, "I can come with you."

Yes, said Everly's heart. *Say, yes.*

She dropped her gaze from his. "You've already helped enough." Then she added quickly, lest he mistake her sincerity for sarcasm, "Honestly, without you I never would have found out what happened to my brother."

"Maybe that's what is bothering me," said Wyatt. "We still really don't know what happened, or why. All we have is a suspect."

She wasn't sure if Wyatt was admitting he thought that Larry was guilty or not. Yet, she decided to question him no further. "I guess knowing who is guilty is enough for me."

Gus pawed the door again, this time with more force.

"You know," he said. "This isn't over. Larry Walker was set up to look guilty, but he's not."

Everly was defeated. "If not Larry," she asked, "then who?"

Wyatt shoved his hand into his pockets and shook

his head. "I'm not sure," said Wyatt. His voice was filled with gravel. Gus whimpered. "I'm sorry for snapping at you. Obviously, we aren't going to agree on any of this."

Everly wasn't sure what to say. She was unable to hold his gaze any longer and looked away.

Gus pawed at the door again.

"I have to take my dog out."

"Go," she said.

"Will you be here when I get back?" he asked.

Everly shook her head.

Wyatt snorted. "Probably for the best."

Then he was gone.

Standing alone in the middle of Wyatt's house, Everly's chest ached. Her throat was raw. Her eyes burned. She recognized the feeling and had come to know it well. It was grief, only this time the loss was Everly's choice.

She had to wonder: What if she chased after Wyatt now? What if she told him that coming to care for him was unexpected and scary? Yet through this whole intense episode, she'd learned you were only guaranteed the day you had and the next one may never come. There was something between Wyatt and Everly, they both knew it. Shouldn't they cling to whatever happiness they could find? Shouldn't they hold on to each other?

Then again, they couldn't even talk about who murdered her brother, the single thing they had in common, without arguing.

Leaning against the wall, Everly knew that her chance with Wyatt had vanished.

Wyatt assumed that Everly would be gone when he got back with Gus. She'd told him as much, and still he hoped that she changed her mind. The house came in to view. Her car was gone, and an emptiness filled his gut.

Why did he care? Everly had burst into his life only a few days before, disrupting his carefully cultivated world. Once again, he had all the solitude he wanted. Funny thing, though—Wyatt now hated the idea of entering a house where nobody was home.

Gus sniffed the ground where Everly's rental car had been parked. He looked to Wyatt and whimpered.

"I know, boy," said Wyatt. "It's just the two of us again."

The dog whined.

Wyatt agreed.

He opened the door and stepped into his house. His one-time refuge felt like a prison. He wandered to the window seat where they'd made love and sat down looking out at the mountains. For the first time in years, Wyatt was left without a direction, or a purpose, for his life.

"Now what?" he asked.

Gus sat in the middle of the kitchen, staring at the counter.

"Breakfast?" asked Wyatt.

The dog barked and thumped his tail in agreement.

Wyatt poured food in Gus's dish and set it on the floor. He should eat something—he hadn't grabbed a bite since lunch yesterday—but his appetite was gone. Leaning against the counter, Wyatt knew that he needed to pass the information he'd gotten from Davis onto Sheriff Haak.

Maybe everyone else was right, and Larry Walker really was guilty. After all, it wouldn't have been the first time Wyatt had made a mistake.

After moving to the desk, he powered up his computer and typed out an email. After hitting Send, he leaned back in his seat. His eye was drawn to the flash drive that held all of the information about the victims.

Assuming that Larry Walker really was the prime suspect, there had to be something that he'd missed. Why had Larry Walker never turned up during the investigation? He knew Everly's prime focus was to find out who'd killed her brother—not examine Larry's psyche, uncover what had driven him to commit all the crimes—but Wyatt wanted to know.

Wyatt inserted the flash drive into his computer and began opening all his files.

He recalled the initial reason they'd suspected the blackjack dealer all those years ago. It was the man's intense interest in the case. In fact, they'd found his face in several photos that had been taken of crowds at a press conference.

Could Larry Walker have been in those crowds as well?

There were a dozen photos, taken at various times

during the investigation, and Wyatt printed them all. Next, he scanned each picture for Larry Walker. Without question, the assumed killer wasn't among those in the crowd.

Wyatt changed tactics and began with the first Las Vegas victim—the one with the connection to Larry via the apartment complex.

Just as a seemingly inconsequential argument had led to Axl Baker's murder, had this man argued with Larry, as well? Was there some insult that had triggered Larry into a murderous rage? And if so, how would Wyatt figure it out all these years later?

He had transcripts of the victim's voice messages sent and received. There were text messages, too. He read them again, even though every message had been scrutinized, and any mention of an altercation would have been flagged as suspicious.

After half an hour, he had nothing to show for his time.

Sitting back in the desk, Wyatt squeezed the bridge of his nose.

Gus was lying in the middle of the room. He lifted his head and looked at Wyatt before flopping back down.

Turning back to the computer, Wyatt opened the saved social-media account for Victim #1. He knew all the pictures before he saw them. There were smiling faces of happy people, oftentimes with drinks in hand. The identities of those in the photos had been tagged.

He moved on to the next picture—this one was

a close-up selfie of the victim in a dark blue shirt. Wyatt expanded the picture, so that it filled the whole screen. In the lower left corner was a detail he hadn't noticed before. What appeared to be the victim's shoulder was actually the top of a head with dark brown hair. On closer inspection, Wyatt found the beginning of a forehead, just a sliver of flesh, at the very bottom of the picture.

A woman? For the moment, he'd assume so.

The photo had been taken at night, as evidenced by the dark surroundings. The backdrop was an adobe wall with an out-of-focus sign. Wyatt expanded the picture, focusing the screen on the sign. He increased the resolution. Only a few words were visible, but they were enough: No Swimming After Midnight. By Order of Grand Canyon Gardens Management.

Wyatt's pulse increased. He had evidence that the photo had been taken at the same place Larry lived. It proved that the victim had been in proximity to the suspected killer.

His next question focused on the woman in the picture. Had she just been passing by and been caught in the photo? Or was the mystery woman supposed to be in the picture and later been edited out?

The sheet of paper Wyatt had scribbled on while talking to Davis had been shoved to the back of the desk, all but forgotten. One word was circled. *Roommate.* Beneath that he'd scribbled two more words: *1 Female.*

Could this woman in the photo with Victim #1

be Larry's roommate? It was a long shot, sure. But sometimes a long shot was the only one you got. Wyatt immediately formed a possible scenario—one that fit all the facts he knew. Larry had a history of violence against women. In Las Vegas, Larry had lived with a woman.

What if the victims weren't connected directly with Larry, but his female roommate? Larry could very easily be a jealous boyfriend or, worse yet, a spurned lover. He knew it was a leap. Yet, Wyatt was ready to make that final jump.

He stared at the picture of Victim #1. Light brown hair. Blue eyes. Bright white smile. He opened another window on his computer and searched for Axl Baker. His professional website topped the search list. A picture of Axl checking his camera was on the first page of his site.

Light brown hair. Blue eyes. Bright white smile. Both men had similar looks and, moreover, they were the kind of guy that women found handsome. Wyatt knew that all the other victims were similarly good-looking, same age, race and gender, and therefore fit the victimology.

But then he remembered the cats. And the trophies from past killings, along with a list of everything that Davis had found.

Wyatt pressed down on the pen. Ink seeped from the tip, leaving a black stain.

Serial killers were ritualistic, he knew. They did things for a reason—and those reasons never change. If Larry had kept personal belongings from his victims in Las Vegas, why hadn't he done the same in Pleasant Pines? Why change?

His house had been thoroughly searched last night. There were no hidden compartments. Nothing linked Larry to victims from Pleasant Pines, or elsewhere.

Then again, that really wasn't the question Wyatt should be asking. Larry Walker didn't fit the typical profile of a serial killer because he wasn't one. He'd been set up, but by who?

If Wyatt's instinct was right, it meant that the real killer was still at large in Pleasant Pines. It also meant that nobody—especially Everly—was safe.

Chapter 13

The sun began creeping upward, changing the sky from red and orange to a light blue. Shadows stretched across the mountainous roads as Everly drove into town. She felt emotionally drained, but she had more to do—namely, get her brother's body home.

Using her cell phone, she contacted the airline and worked out the details for the transport of Axl's body. Next, she contacted a funeral home in Cheyenne that advertised early morning hours. She hired them to take Axl to the airport. By the time she finished both calls it was 7:15 a.m. Even though it was early, Everly had several things to accomplish before leaving Pleasant Pines.

Finally, she needed to contact the sheriff and file

the official paperwork that would release Axl's body. She doubted that Haak would be in the office yet and it left her with some time to kill. Everly hadn't been worried about food at Wyatt's house and now, she needed some breakfast. Turning her car onto Main Street, she found the diner Wyatt had taken her to the other day, Sally's on Main.

She tried not to think about Wyatt, or the pie he'd sworn by. The thought came to her, anyway, and she smiled.

Everly pulled into a parking space and walked to the front door. Taking a booth at the back of the room, she picked up a menu.

Sally, the waitress, approached with a coffeepot in hand. "Care for some high-test?" she asked.

Everly flipped over her cup. "Please."

"What can I get for you?"

"Two eggs over-easy, wheat toast and a side of fruit," she said.

Sally wrote down the order. "There was a lot happening at the inn last night. Do you know anything about that?"

"Too much," said Everly.

"Will Wyatt be meeting you? It's good to see him out and about. He's alone too much," she added.

Everly wasn't sure if she should be offended that the server assumed they were a couple. Or if she should be sad that they weren't. "It's just me for breakfast. I'm heading back to Chicago this morning," Everly said.

"Well, we hope you'll come back soon."

Everly smiled. "Thanks."

Sure, Pleasant Pines didn't have the busy lifestyle or attractions that could be found in Chicago. But what it lacked in museums and shopping, it made up for in kindness.

That sense of community was rare. Beyond caring for Wyatt, had Everly fallen in love with Wyoming?

Maybe there was a middle ground for them after all. Perhaps they didn't have to be either recluses in the boonies or live a fast-paced life in the big city. She pulled her phone from her purse and brought up Wyatt's contact info. She'd slunk away without saying goodbye or even thank you. She owed him a call.

Without another thought, she hit the phone icon. The call went straight to voice mail. Damn. Everly sat up taller, refusing to lose her nerve again.

"Wyatt, it's me." She paused. "I hate how things ended between us. I wanted to apologize for leaving while you were out. I have a flight back to Chicago this afternoon but will be in town until Axl's body is released." Everly knew she was rambling. She let out a deep breath and tried again. "If you get this message…well, I'd like to see you. I'm at the diner now."

Everly ended the call, just as Sally delivered breakfast. "Here you go, hon."

She ate quickly, and when done with her meal, Everly checked her phone. Wyatt hadn't called. He hadn't texted. She didn't know if he'd even heard her message. Or maybe he had heard the message but decided not to call her back. Maybe he didn't really want her to stay in Wyoming. If that was the case, then it was best if she left town.

The waitress approached with the coffeepot. "Need a warm-up?"

"No thanks," said Everly.

Meeting with the sheriff was the final thing that Everly needed to do. Once her brother's body was released, she could take him back to Chicago. She was leaving Pleasant Pines, yet Everly knew that memories of the town—and Wyatt in particular—would stay with her long after she'd gone.

"You wouldn't happen to know what time Sheriff Haak gets to the office?" Everly asked.

"He usually doesn't show up until half past eight," said Sally.

Everly glanced at the clock. She had almost another hour to wait.

"Anything else?" the waitress asked.

Sally seemed to know everything about everyone. "Any idea what time Darcy Owens goes into work at the inn?"

"Her shift usually begins at ten o'clock." Sally shrugged. "I only know because she sometimes stops in to get coffee and a bear claw first."

Maybe the cordiality of life in a small town was beginning to rub off on Everly. She felt compelled to thank Darcy personally before leaving town.

A quick internet search gave Everly an address for Darcy's home. Sure, it was early, but without Darcy's initial lead, she'd never know what had happened to Axl—despite Wyatt's misgivings. After a quick visit, Everly would be done with Pleasant Pines and she wouldn't look back.

Pleasant Pines wasn't a large town, but Everly needed her GPS to find Darcy Owens's house. The street was filled with small homes and neatly kept yards. Parking at the curb, Everly hoped that an un-invited visit wasn't considered rude. After turning off her engine, Everly walked up the path and rang the bell.

A sheer curtain was drawn over the front window and lights were on in the room beyond. She waited. There was no answer. A carport was off to the side of the small house and a sedan was parked in the drive. Someone was home, she knew.

She knocked on the door. Her knuckles grazed the wood and the door creaked open slightly. Everly re-alized that the handle hadn't been latched, and now, the door was ajar.

"Sorry," she said loudly. "I didn't realize."

She heard a woman's voice—it was faint, but dis-tinct. Had she been told to come in?

"It's Everly Baker," she called out, "from the hotel. I wanted to thank you. Mind if I come in?"

There it was again—the woman's voice, with a quick laugh. What had she said?

Everly pushed the door open farther. There was a small entryway, covered in linoleum tile. It was con-nected to a living room, decorated in light blue and sunny yellow. "Darcy?" she said. "I hate to intrude, but I'm leaving for Chicago in a little while and I wanted to thank you for all your help."

Beyond the living room was another room. From where she stood, Everly could see a ceiling light ablaze and the edge of a counter. The kitchen?

Everly stepped into the house and shut the door. "Hello?"

She followed the voice. Like she had guessed from the entryway, the person was in a kitchen. The counters were pristine and white. The wooden cabinets gleamed in the overhead light. The only thing that seemed out of place was the cluttered kitchen table, and the TV that sat atop the refrigerator.

A morning newscast played, and two female anchors discussed the day's weather. Everly immediately recognized the voice she assumed had belonged to Darcy.

No matter how friendly people seemed in Pleasant Pines, coming in to someone's home without permission was rude—or worse, criminal. It probably didn't really matter, though, as long as she could sneak away.

Then she saw it and froze.

The metallic taste of panic coated her tongue. She reached for it, but her hand was unsteady. Her finger grazed the cold, metal casing, and she lifted it from the table. Everly turned the camera around and looked at the bottom—there, just as she knew it would be, was an inscription.

To Axl on your 30th B-day
Capture the best of life
Love, Everly

For a moment, Everly was back in Axl's hotel room at the Pleasant Pines Inn. This time, the memory was complete. In that moment, there had been a whisper of sound behind her and she had turned. In the mirror, she caught the glimpse of a figure. Without question, it was Darcy Owens.

"Everly?" Darcy Owens stood on the threshold of the kitchen. She wore a robe. Her hair was wet, and she held a towel. She looked stunned. "What are you doing here?"

Darcy's gaze dropped from Everly's face to her hands and the camera she held. The smile faltered, and Darcy narrowed her eyes.

"You," Everly growled. Her face was hot, and she began to sweat. "It was you all along. You killed my brother. You killed them *all*."

Wide-eyed, Darcy gaped. "I don't know what you're talking about."

"You don't? Well, I imagine that Sheriff Haak will be interested in why you have my brother's camera in your house." Everly stepped forward, ready to brush past Darcy.

The other woman blocked the way, trapping Everly in the kitchen. "I wish you hadn't come here, Everly. Because you aren't going to leave alive."

After running the social-media picture of Victim #1 through several programs, Wyatt discovered a few important points. First, the photo had been cropped before being posted to social media. With his equipment, he couldn't return the picture to its original form.

What he needed was a more advanced computer, like the one at Rocky Mountain Justice.

He opened his phone's contact app. After finding Marcus Jones's info, he placed the call.

Jones answered on the second ring. "Wyatt? What's up?"

Wyatt paused. He knew they all assumed that Larry Walker was the killer. He knew that he'd followed all the clues, leading them to a perfect suspect. Yet, he also knew he'd been wrong.

His heart stilled.

Wyatt refused to hide anymore while terrified of making another mistake.

"Wyatt?" Jones asked. "You there?"

"It wasn't Larry. He was set up."

"If this is your idea of a joke," said Marcus, "it's a bad one."

"I wish I was kidding, but Larry isn't our doer." Wyatt gave a quick rundown of the Las Vegas find, the hidden compartment with the mummified cats and the trophies from previous victims. He pointed out that nothing of that nature had been found in Larry's Pleasant Pines residence.

"People change," said Marcus. "Even sickos."

"More than most people, serial killers are consistent. True, sometime circumstances vary from one kill to the next, but that has more to do with opportunity and the victims than it does the killer. Their modus operandi is pretty reliable. That's been true of this killer, as well."

"But he lived in that apartment," said Marcus. "You can't deny that the trophies were found in his home."

"According to a neighbor in Las Vegas, Larry had a roommate," said Wyatt. "No other tenants were listed on the lease, so we don't have a name. We do know that the roommate was a female."

"Tell me you have more on this case. Maybe another suspect?"

"I have a picture from the first Las Vegas victim. I think Larry's roommate might be in the photo."

"Can we get an identity?"

"Not with the way it is now. It's just a little bit of a woman's scalp. But I can tell that the photo's been edited."

"And you're wondering if you can use RMJ's equipment again?"

"Exactly," said Wyatt.

"How long before you can get to the office?"

"I'll see you in fifteen minutes," he said and ended the call.

Wyatt saved what he had on the flash drive and shoved it into his pocket. He placed all the printed photos into a file folder and grabbed those, as well. He reached for his phone before slipping on his vest. He jogged to his truck and started the engine. The tires kicked up gravel as Wyatt raced down the driveway. He turned hard to the right as he hit the pavement. The big engine revved and the truck fishtailed as he sped down the road.

Everly was trapped. Darcy stood on the threshold, blocking the only exit. Everly's heartbeat slammed into her chest and bile rose in the back of her throat.

Clutching Axl's camera, she dropped her shoulder and ran straight at Darcy, crashing into the other woman. Darcy toppled back, slamming into the floor. Everly rushed forward, focusing on nothing other than the door and freedom.

Darcy reached for her, catching her ankle. Her foot twisted, a bolt of pain shot up her leg and she stumbled. Darcy wrenched Everly's leg upward, and she fell to the floor.

Her chin slammed into the carpet and her teeth cracked together. She crawled forward, determined to escape.

Darcy pounced, scrambling on top of Everly and pinning her down. From behind, she gripped Everly's throat. Still clutching the camera, Everly swung out. The metal-and-plastic casing connected hard. Everly felt the satisfying reverberations travel from her hand to her shoulder.

Darcy's grip faltered and Everly inched forward, freeing herself. She flipped to her back, just as Darcy lunged again. On instinct alone, Everly lifted her foot and drove her heel forward. The sole of her boot connected with Darcy's mouth.

The other woman's blond head snapped back and Everly was on her feet. She reached for the door handle, her fingers brushing the cold metal. Pain erupted in her scalp as Darcy grabbed a handful of Everly's hair and twisted.

Holding tight to the camera, Everly swung out, catching the killer in the cheek. Darcy gave a feral wail and fell over, her hand full of Everly's hair.

Everly ignored her throbbing head and her burning throat, focusing only on freedom. She lunged forward. A hard shove came from behind, slamming Everly into the door. The handle gouged her side, and she cried out with pain.

She drove her elbow back. It connected with Darcy's middle and the other woman let out a wheeze.

Everly gripped the handle and turned.

Darcy chopped Everly's wrist with her fist. "You aren't going anywhere, bitch," she snarled.

Everly whirled around. Darcy looked wild. Her eyes were glassy. Her teeth were stained red, and a trickle of blood ran from her lip.

Everly had to get out of the house, now. She pressed her back to the door for leverage and kicked out, hitting Darcy square in the chest. The other woman flew back, crashing into a coffee table, her head slamming into the glass top.

Darcy didn't get up.

Everly opened the door and she drew in a lungful of fresh air. She took a step across the threshold, her car in sight. She'd call Wyatt and the sheriff for help, tell them what she'd discovered. And she'd tell Wyatt that he'd been right all along—that the real killer had been hiding in plain sight.

Then pain exploded in Everly's skull. For a moment, her stomach reeled, and she only saw red. Then her knees gave out and she dropped to the ground.

Then there was only blackness.

Wyatt drove and wondered if he was pursuing yet another dead end. Even if they could return his copy of the picture to its original form, what would it get them? A face without a name? After pulling up in front of the RMJ safe house, Wyatt killed the engine. He stepped onto the curb and the front door opened. Marcus stood on the threshold.

"The camera down the street picked you up as soon as you rounded the corner," Marcus said.

"That's impressive tech you have," Wyatt said as he strode up the walkway. "Hopefully, it can help us with this." He removed the flash drive from his pocket and held it up.

"I have confidence in my team," said Marcus. "Come on in."

Wyatt followed Marcus into the house. Even with its state-of-the-art recognition software and impenetrable accesses getting inside took only seconds.

"This way." Marcus opened a door to Wyatt's right.

They were back in the conference room. Three people sat around the table. Wyatt recognized two of them from last night at the Pleasant Pines Inn, when the kitchen had been teeming with law-enforcement officers of all kinds.

After shaking hands with RMJ operatives Luis

Martinez and Julia McCloud, Wyatt dropped into a chair at the end of the table.

Martinez gestured to a dark haired woman in her fifties and said, "Wyatt, this is Katarina." She lifted a hand in acknowledgment.

Marcus continued, "She's our communications expert and hopefully the person who can recover your photograph." Then to Katarina, he said, "This is Wyatt Thornton. He used to work the FBI's behavioral-science unit. He thinks there might be a problem with designating Larry Walker as the Las Vegas and Pleasant Pines killer."

How many years had passed since Wyatt gave his last briefing? It was in Las Vegas and they were hunting the same killer he now faced. Filled with confidence, he'd stood at the head of a conference table and laid out all the facts knew. They had a suspect— but a single problem. The man had an alibi for one of the murders.

Perhaps, one colleague had surmised, the suspect had committed most of the crimes—just not all of them. A copycat killer, he had suggested.

Wyatt had assured everyone in the room that there was no copycat killer in their case, and their serial killer was responsible for all the killings. Besides, each victim had been found with the same calling card, that half of a two-dollar bill. It meant that each man had been killed by a single person.

It was then that Wyatt's supervisor had spoken up. People in Las Vegas were afraid. The task force needed to show progress. The suspect would be arrested, and, moreover, investigative resources would be turned to disproving the alibi.

At the time, Wyatt had balked at the plan. To him, it was wrong to let an innocent man languish in jail—plain and simple.

In the end, Wyatt was overruled.

The next day, a local reporter had discovered the alibi and Wyatt was thrown under the bus. Some days, he could still feel the tread marks on his back.

All those years ago, Wyatt placed his faith in his colleagues, and in the end, he'd been betrayed.

The operatives from RMJ were basically strangers. Was it prudent to trust anyone, especially people he didn't know?

Then Everly came to mind. If he could trust her, he could take a chance now. Besides, he'd asked them for help. If he wasn't willing to share what he knew, Wyatt should just go back to his house and never leave again.

"I have a picture of the first victim in Las Vegas taken at the apartment complex where Larry Walker lived. It was cropped before being posted on social media, but another person was in the photo. I want to know who she is."

"Do you think she's an accomplice?" Martinez asked.

"Or a victim?" It was Julia who spoke.

"To be honest, I don't know if she's either—or neither. But if this is Larry's roommate, she can tell us something about what happened."

"If you have the photo on a drive, I can get to work," Katarina said.

"Sure do." Wyatt placed the flash drive on the table and slid it toward the woman.

She opened a black leather portfolio that held a wireless keyboard. After hitting a few keys, a screen lowered from the ceiling. She inserted the flash drive into a USB port in the table. A list of all the files appeared on the screen, the letters more than a foot high.

"It's under social-media photo number one," Wyatt said.

Katarina opened the picture.

"Can you get it back to the original file?"

Katarina tapped on the keyboard. "It'll take a while," she said, "but I can get something."

Julia scooted next to Katarina and the women began to talk in hushed tones. Wyatt only caught a few words, but it was enough to know that they were working on a strategy to get a complete picture.

He turned to Marcus. "What's next?"

"I think that we should investigate in-house and see what turns up. There's a substantial case that makes Larry Walker our killer. I have to wonder, what if you're wrong now?"

Acid roiled in Wyatt's gut. It was just like last time. His phone vibrated, saving Wyatt from saying something he'd later regret—or worse, saying nothing, and regretting it now.

He pulled the phone from his pocket and looked

at the screen. Everly had left a voice message more than an hour ago. "Damn," he cursed.

"Everything okay?" Marcus asked.

"I got a call, but it didn't show up until now," he said.

"Take it in the hall if you want," said Marcus.

Wyatt left the room and opened his voice-mail app. "Wyatt, it's me," Everly said. "I hate how things ended between us. I wanted to apologize for leaving while you were out. I have a flight back to Chicago later this morning but will be in town for a few hours." She let out a deep breath. "If you get this message…well, I'd like to see you again. Give me a call. Maybe we can meet up. I'm at the diner now."

Everly was at the diner—and more important, she wanted to see him. Yet, he couldn't leave RMJ, not until he found out who was in the picture. Hours could pass before they had an image. By then, Everly would be gone.

Was he really willing to miss his last chance to see her—even if she only wanted to say goodbye?

Chapter 14

Wyatt stood in the hall, just outside of the conference room. He listened to Everly's message a second time, trying to determine her feelings from the tone of her voice. There was nothing.

The conference-room door opened, and Wyatt turned at the sound.

Marcus stood on the threshold. "Katarina just told me that this is going to take a while. She's not even sure if there's much more of the picture to recover."

Disappointment rose in Wyatt's throat. He swallowed it down. Then again, the delay allowed him to leave RMJ and deal with more important things, like Everly. "I need to be somewhere," he said. "Text me if you get anything."

Wyatt could've walked the four blocks to Main Street and the diner, but he took his truck, parking right by the front door.

He peered through the window and saw several patrons. No sign of Everly, though. She was gone. The instinct to hunt, to find her, kicked in and he opened the front door. The salty scent of bacon frying mixed with the deep, dark smell of coffee.

"Morning, hon," said Sally. "Take a seat and I'll be right with you."

"Actually, I'm looking for someone. The woman I was here with the other day—"

She interrupted. "You mean Everly?"

He should have known. Word traveled fast in a small town. "Yes. Have you seen her?"

"She was here about an hour ago, had breakfast and left."

"Did she say anything about where she was going? Was she leaving town straight away?"

"She didn't say anything about leaving just yet, but she did ask when Sheriff Haak got in to his office."

"So, she's with the sheriff," said Wyatt. "Thanks."

Wyatt pivoted and pulled the door open. Cold mountain air rushed in to the small diner.

"Wait," called Sally. "Sheriff Haak hasn't come in for his morning coffee yet, so he's not gotten to work. Everly did mention something else," Sally said.

Wyatt's curiosity was piqued. "She did? What?"

"Everly wanted to thank Darcy Owens for being so kind."

"Darcy? The desk clerk from the inn?"

"That's the one."

Finding Darcy's address would be simple enough, he'd just look it up when he got back to RMJ.

"Thanks, Sally," said Wyatt. "You're the best."

After stepping onto the street, he opted not to wait that long, and opened his phone's internet browser and found an address for Darcy Owens. It was only a few blocks away.

While walking to his truck, his phone began to ring. He glanced at the screen before answering the call. "Marcus," he asked. "Anything new?"

"We have a photo, but the resolution isn't great. I'm not even sure that we can enter the picture into recognition software. I'm sending it to you right now, anyway."

"I'll take a look and get back to you," said Wyatt as he backed onto the street.

The phone buzzed with an incoming text. Wyatt ignored it until he pulled up at a stop sign. He glanced at the phone—and froze. The photo was blurry, as if the subject had been moving while the picture was being taken, but he could just make out the resemblance.

Marcus was wrong. There was definitely something familiar about the photo. "Damn," he cursed.

He'd been so sure that there was a connection—and he was right.

Dropping his foot on the accelerator, the truck

shot forward. The file of photos dropped from the seat and scattered across the floorboard. Pulling to the side of the road, Wyatt bent down to retrieve the pictures.

There it was—one face out of hundreds. Sure, the hair color was different, but the face was the same.

In the crowd of onlookers was Darcy Owens.

He flipped through each picture in rapid succession. Despite the fact the she'd donned a disguise—glasses, hats, once a green wig—he found her face in each one.

For Wyatt, suddenly all the questions, and all the foggy and dissatisfying answers, became clear. The serial killer's hesitation to take Everly's life made sense—if the killer was female. The fact that the male victims were easily lured from the hotel also made sense—if the killer was female.

In fact, poisoning had been the preferred method of female killers for centuries. And in reality, isn't that what she had done? Poisoned her victims before leaving them for dead?

It was Darcy who enlightened them all about Larry Walker's fight with Axl Baker—thus providing a suspect. It was also Darcy who sent Larry to the meeting with a tray full of coffee, just as his guilt was being discussed. No doubt, Darcy predicted that Larry would run, making him look guilty.

Then again, if he was innocent, why would Larry commit suicide?

What if he was deeply in her thrall? Wyatt could easily imagine Darcy convincing Larry to stage a hanging. Perhaps promises were made to find Larry in time to save his life. Perhaps she convinced Larry to kill himself—telling him it was the only way she'd avoid jail time—and he had agreed.

Time began again. And Wyatt knew one thing for sure. He needed to get to Everly, now—or she was as good as dead.

Accelerating around the corner, Wyatt pulled onto the narrow street filled with small houses. Like the beam shining from a lighthouse on a stormy sea, sun glinted off the windshield of Everly's rental car. Yet, he didn't relax—he wouldn't relax, not even for a second, until Everly was safe.

He parked across the street. After opening the glove box, he removed his SIG Sauer and slid it into the back of his pants. Wyatt considered contacting Marcus or Sheriff Haak. Then again, he wasn't going to wait for backup to arrive, much less take the minutes needed to make a call.

He hustled up the walkway. The door was ajar, and he pushed it open. The hinges creaked, as the door swung inward. Wyatt stepped into the room and his heart dropped.

Shattered glass was scattered all over the floor, several shards covered in blood. Wyatt kneeled next to the table. The blood was viscous—not wet, not dry. He'd guess that the whole episode had taken place an hour ago, no more.

Standing, he surveyed the rest of the room. A snarl of red hair was stark against the white carpet. There was a tiny piece of scalp attached.

A venomous rage burned in his veins. He would make Darcy Owens pay for the pain she'd caused Everly. That emotion was quickly replaced with icy fear. What if Darcy really had killed her this time?

He wiped a shaking hand down his face. He wouldn't do Everly any good if he let his imagination rule his intellect. He needed to assess the situation—and then act.

Obviously, there had been a struggle. Had Everly somehow figured out that Darcy was involved in Axl's death and confronted the other woman? Or was Darcy—knowing her own guilt—suspicious of Everly's unannounced visit? In the end, the answer to those questions didn't matter. For Wyatt, all that counted was who had won.

Removing his gun, Wyatt stayed low as he moved down the hall. There was a door to the left. Gripping his gun, he pushed open the door and slid into the room. It was a bedroom with an adjacent bathroom.

The bed was unmade, the closet door closed. At first glance, there was nothing amiss. He opened the closet and pulled all the clothes from the rack. Nothing. Nothing under the bed or hidden between the mattress and box spring. The bathroom was likewise empty.

There was another room across the hall.

Wyatt stood on the threshold, his heartbeat hammering. He wanted to find her, needed to see Everly—unharmed. He knew that his hope was foolishness and yet, he felt as if by sheer will alone, he could make it a reality.

He pushed open the door. It was a second bedroom. Bed. Table. Desk. He conducted a quick, systematic, but fruitless search. None of the rooms bore the scars from an attack. No overturned tables or broken lamps. It looked as if the fight had been contained to the living room, as if it happened when someone tried to enter—or maybe it was leave.

How could he have left Everly alone? He cursed his pride and moved to the last room to be searched. A shattered camera sat near the doorway separating the living room from the kitchen. Taking a knee, Wyatt examined the rubble. Engraved into the bottom was a note:

To Axl on your 30th B-day
Capture the best of life
Love, Everly

The final puzzle piece snapped into place. Wyatt didn't take time to either congratulate or berate himself. This was proof that Everly was in the hands of a killer. He had to act quickly. Wyatt's instinct was to rush out, but go where?

Standing in the middle of Darcy's living room, he tried to get a sense of what everything meant. It was a cozy house. Yet, Wyatt knew that Darcy was far from being the homey type. That meant it was an act and this place was a stage, but for whom?

There had to be a connection between Las Vegas and Pleasant Pines.

Like a sun cresting the horizon, he understood

that there was only one thing that would bring Darcy Owens to Wyoming—it was him. It had been Wyatt all along.

Darcy was playing a sick game, and he was her unwitting opponent.

It was why the killings stopped when he left Las Vegas.

It was why a body was dumped at the old schoolhouse, where he would be the one to find it.

It was also how he knew exactly where she'd taken Everly.

Knowing where to look was a good thing, but he'd never be able to catch Darcy unaware. What Wyatt needed was help. Taking the phone from his pocket, he placed a call.

"Wyatt," said Sheriff Haak as he answered. "I was just reading your email. It looks like you finally caught your man."

"Larry Walker's not the serial killer—and I need your help," said Wyatt. He felt the seconds ticking by with each beat of his heart. He rushed from the empty house to his truck and started the engine. "I don't have time to explain everything right now, but it was Darcy Owens all along. She was Larry's roommate in Las Vegas, so she'd have access to the apartment."

"His roommate? I don't get it? Last night, it sounded like she barely knew him."

"It was a lie," he said. Tires squealing, he pulled away from the curb. "We need to act now. She's got Everly."

"Whoa there," said the sheriff. "Hold your horses one second and tell me what's happening. How's Everly involved, exactly?"

Wyatt took a deep breath to steel himself. "I went looking for Everly at Darcy's house. There's evidence of a confrontation and there's blood on the floor. And…her brother's missing camera. It's here."

Wyatt felt desperation threaten to choke him, but he tamped it down. He had one goal—and he wouldn't be distracted by emotion. "Everly's car is still in front of Darcy's house but both of the women are gone."

"Tell me what you need," said Sheriff Haak. "And I'll do it."

"I think I know where Darcy's taken Everly. They're at the old schoolhouse. I'm going there now and need backup. Can you meet me?"

"I'll do you one better," said Haak. "My house is less than five minutes away from your property, so I'll get there first."

Wyatt ended the call and placed another. Marcus Jones answered. "Hello?"

Not wasting any time on pleasantries, Wyatt began, "Darcy Owens is the killer and she's kidnapped Everly. I think she's taken her to the old schoolhouse."

For his part, Marcus asked few questions while Wyatt briefed him as he drove.

"The sheriff should be there soon. I'll call you

once I hear something, but it's going to take all of us if we're going to catch Darcy Owens."

"I'll round up the team from RMJ and we'll have your back ASAP." He hesitated. "Good luck, Wyatt."

"Thanks," said Wyatt. "But I don't need luck. For me, this is personal."

Everly's head was throbbing. She swallowed, but her throat was tight, as if a weight pressed down on her neck. Her eyes burned, yet she pried her lids open. A bright light shone in her face. With a curse, she screwed her eyes shut again. She tried to rub her neck, but her hands didn't—or more accurately, couldn't—move.

Suddenly awake, Everly remembered finding Axl's camera at Darcy's house. And then, the fight to escape—a fight Everly had lost. She pulled at her arms again. They were pinned behind her back and her wrists were bound. Fighting the pain in her head, she studied her surroundings. In an instant, Everly knew exactly where she was—in the old schoolhouse on Wyatt's property.

A thick rope was wound around her neck, tightening each time she drew a breath.

"Careful..." A woman's voice came from the shadows. "You are perched on top of a wobbly stool, and you've got a noose around your neck. A very precarious place. If you struggle too much, if you try to get down, if you budge that stool at all, you'll end up hanged."

Darcy stepped into the light. A trickle of blood

had dried on her cheek. Her bottom lip was swollen and split. The white of one eye had turned bright red.

Everly grew cold as she listened to Darcy. Her knees shook and the stool beneath her began to sway. The rope tightened further, cutting off all her breath. Everly's hands and feet went numb. Her heart raced as panic began to claim her.

No. She couldn't lose it. Not now.

Everly forced herself to stand still and focus on one thing: survival. She held her breath as the stool gradually steadied and she slowly exhaled. "What have you done?"

"Me?" Darcy placed a hand on her chest. "What have *I* done? The question you should be asking is what have *you* done? Why are you here?"

Everly swallowed. The stool teetered, tightening the rope. "Okay. Why am I here?"

"First, it's because you are really stupid. You can't take a clue, can you?"

Everly didn't think Darcy expected an answer, and she didn't give one.

"I could have killed you twice. First, at the hotel while you explored your brother's room. Then the other night at Wyatt's house. I didn't, because I don't kill women. You aren't the problem. Still, if you slip from this stool and die, well, it's your own fault, isn't it?"

Everly's eyes burned with angry tears. Darcy had constructed the perfect trap and there was no way Everly could escape, much less survive. No matter what scenario she turned over in her mind, she just couldn't figure a way out of this. Her only hope was to connect with Darcy, maybe talk to her—woman-to-woman. "Cut me loose, Darcy. We both know you really don't want to see anything happen to me. Like you said, you could have killed me before, but you didn't."

"Don't presume to know what's in my heart," said Darcy. Her lips twisted into a snarl and spittle flew from her mouth. Rushing to Everly's side, she knocked over the stool.

For a moment, Everly hung in the air. Then all her weight was on her neck. Her throat collapsed. Her eyes bulged. Her legs thrashed. She couldn't breathe. Her heart felt as if it would explode in her chest.

"You should have left when you had the chance," said Darcy. "You had your killer—Larry, that idiot—and you and Wyatt would have lived the rest of your days thinking that you'd solved the crime of the century. But no." Darcy retrieved the stool and slid it under Everly's feet. She loosened the noose just a little. "You couldn't leave well enough alone, could you?"

Everly settled her tiptoes on the stool and drew in deep breaths. "Why kill me? You said that I wasn't the problem."

"Not at first," said Darcy. "Did you know that when Wyoming was a territory, thievery was a capital offense? When this building was used, a person could be hanged for stealing something of value."

The question made no sense. Obviously, Darcy

had a point to make. What Everly needed was a way to escape. Her only plan—her only option—was to play along. "I didn't know that."

"I think it's a just punishment. Don't you?"

"No," said Everly. She had to fight to keep her voice steady. "I don't. Property isn't the same as a life."

"A thief denies a person of their possessions. They take from someone what's rightfully theirs."

"I haven't taken anything from you," said Everly.

"Haven't you?"

"The camera? That belonged to my brother. Why did he have to die? What did he steal from you?"

"Him," Darcy growled. "You stole him from me."

"Axl? I didn't take my brother from you," Everly said. Even as she spoke, Everly knew her guess was wrong.

"Your brother?" Darcy snorted. "He was nothing to me, only a means to an end. You stole Wyatt Thornton. And now, you have to pay for your crime."

Carl Haak dropped his foot onto the accelerator. The truck shot forward, pressing him back into the seat. The tires kicked up gravel as he raced down the dirt road to the old schoolhouse. His siren's scream filled the silent morning and his lights cast shadows of red and blue across the landscape.

Over forty years of law-enforcement experience had taught Carl a thing or two. The number one lesson was that sometimes a big show of force—

lights, sirens, guns—ended many violent situations peaceably.

He pulled up next to the schoolhouse. A small, gray sedan was parked nearby, and he immediately recognized it as belonging to Darcy Owens.

She was there and if Wyatt's report was right... so was Everly. His heartbeat spiked and sweat began to drip from his brow. He didn't have time to think of a plan. Slamming on the breaks, the sheriff skidded to a stop next to Darcy's car. He turned off the ignition and pocketed the keys before opening the door. While jumping down, he drew his sidearm and held it at the ready.

Carl's breath came in short, ragged gasps and he rushed toward the little building. He pressed his back to the wall and glanced into the single room. He withdrew just as quickly and tried to make sense of what he'd seen.

Everly Baker had been hanging by her neck. A rope was tied to a thick, wooden beam in the ceiling. Was he too late? No. She stood on a stool. Her eyes had been opened wide. What else had been in the room? Or rather, had he caught a glimpse of Darcy Owens?

Sheriff Haak exhaled. Aside from Everly, the room had been empty. No doubt, Darcy Owens had heard his approach and fled the scene. Gun drawn, he stepped into the old schoolhouse.

"Sheriff," said Everly. Her voice was raspy. "Be careful."

He ignored her warning. Holstering his gun,

Carl rushed to Everly's side. The noose was growing tight around her neck as she grew agitated, and she stood on a stool that wobbled, one leg shorter than the others.

Carl circled Everly and stopped at her back. "Your hands are tied together," he said. "Let me at least get you loose." He didn't bother to add that with free hands she could grab the rope and save herself from strangulation if things went from bad to worse. After removing a utility knife from his pants pocket, he sliced into the rope.

The stool wobbled with each swipe of the blade.

Everly screamed in pain as the noose tightened, digging deeper into her neck. Carl grabbed her legs, supporting her weight and keeping her still. The stool remained steady and he released Everly's legs. Sweat dripped down Carl's back and his pulse pounded. "I got to get you down from there somehow, but this isn't working."

"Darcy heard your truck approaching and left. She might be watching us even now. You need to leave me here," she said, "and go."

"I'm not going anywhere," said Carl. "Not until I get you down and take you with me."

He glanced over his shoulder. There was nothing—and no one—in the room. "I have a ladder in my truck. Once we get you on something solid, I can get that rope from your neck. Hold tight and I'll be right back."

He turned for the door, stopping to peer outside. Aside from his truck and Darcy's car, there was nothing beyond mountains and blue sky.

He knew that Everly was right about Darcy—she couldn't have gotten far, not without her own car at least. Wily as she was, Carl figured that Darcy was a smart woman and wouldn't risk a standoff with an armed man. Still, Carl kept low as he ran to his truck. He jerked open the door and reached behind the driver's seat. He grasped the folding ladder he had stored there and pulled it from his truck. Not bothering to shut the door, Carl turned back to the old schoolhouse.

Carl kept low and moved at a brisk pace. He crossed the threshold and held up the folding ladder. "I got it," he said. "You'll be down in a jiff."

Everly's expression changed from wide-eyed worry to white-faced horror. She opened her mouth, but there was no sound.

Carl heard a sharp crack, like the snap of a whip. The sound was followed by a whiff of cordite carried on the breeze. A hot pain shot through his bicep. Carl's arm went numb and the little ladder slipped from his grasp, tumbling to the hard ground with a clatter. Carl's gaze moved to his hand. Blood dripped from his fingertips. The front of his shirt was wet and sticky. A black stain spread across his chest.

There was another pop. Another whiff of cordite and pain hit him again from behind, striking his shoulder and spinning him around.

Darcy held the shotgun Carl had left in his truck. She pulled back on the stock, chambering another round. A blaze erupted from the barrel and Carl was knocked backward by the force of the slug. He fell, and as the ground rushed up to meet him, he could only think that he'd set his retirement date two weeks too late.

Chapter 15

Wyatt stopped his truck half a mile from the old schoolhouse. He didn't know what he'd find and needed more intel before rushing ahead. Peering through a set of binoculars, he surveyed the scene. From his vantage point, Wyatt couldn't see the front door, only the back wall and a corner. Yet, Sheriff Haak's truck and a gray sedan—most likely belonging to Darcy—were visible from where he stood.

He pulled out his phone and placed a call.

"Marcus," he said. "I'm here. Where are you?"

"We're on our way. Less than ten minutes out. Do you have Everly? Or Darcy?"

"Not yet, but I know where they are." He then gave a brief description of what he'd seen. "I'm going in on foot, but I'm going to need cleanup."

"Don't you mean backup?"

"I'm not waiting another second to save Everly," he said and ended the call. Wyatt pocketed the phone and returned to his truck. Removing his AR-15 from the rack, he loaded a clip of twenty-eight bullets.

If Darcy was nearby—and he assumed that she was—he needed the element of surprise. Still, he wanted to make good time and veered from the road, using the surrounding brush as cover. He'd gone less than a hundred yards when he heard it and drew up short.

A gunshot. Once. Twice.

No. Three bullets had been fired in quick succession.

His heart ceased to beat as a vision of Everly's lifeless body came to mind. Once he'd gone down that dark road in his imagination, he could conceive of nothing else. He had to get to her, to save her, to protect her. To convince Everly that he did want to be with her, whether that meant here in Wyoming or joining her back in Chicago. Nothing mattered more than being by her side.

But first, he had to keep her alive.

The hell with being sneaky—Wyatt held tight to the assault rifle and sprinted toward the old schoolhouse. He rounded the building as Darcy Owens came out of the front door.

For a moment, they only stared at each other, neither of them daring to move or speak.

"You're too late," said Darcy. She held a shotgun, the barrel pointed down.

"Drop the gun," he said.

"I'd never hurt you," she said, placing the gun on the ground. Standing, she said, "They're both dead—the sheriff and your girlfriend. I shot him and hanged her. You can shoot me, too. But it won't bring them back—any of them."

He'd heard the gunfire. Why shouldn't he believe Darcy? A burning rage filled Wyatt's chest. Leveling the assault rifle at Darcy, he asked, "Give me one reason why I shouldn't kill you now?"

"Because I did this for *you*," she said. "I killed them *all* for you."

Of all the things that Wyatt expected to hear, that wasn't it. The complete nonsensicalness of her statement stole his breath and left him nauseated.

"This has nothing to do with me."

"Oh, really?" She laughed. "Let me ask you this, Wyatt? Does anything make you feel more alive than hunting a killer? I gave all of that to you. The adrenaline. The danger. The focus. Admit it—it's better than sex."

"I'm not admitting anything to you, Darcy."

"Aren't you proud of me? Don't you think I was clever for fooling them all for so long?"

"I think you're sick," he said. "You've hurt a lot of people. You need to be in prison."

A look of hurt crossed Darcy's face, only to be quickly replaced by a placid expression. "You don't mean that. I know you."

"I don't know you. You definitely don't know me."

"Oh, don't I?"

It was a taunt, nothing more—and yet, Wyatt couldn't help but feel a disturbing stab of accuracy to her statement. She had found him, after all. More than that, she knew exactly how to orchestrate her killings to get him involved in the investigation. He hated to think that Darcy had studied him with the same vigor he'd used to analyze her.

She spoke again. "I watched you in Las Vegas and even knew when you'd arrested the wrong man. I gave you the tip exonerating him. I knew you'd let him go. But you didn't. That was a mistake. I wasn't going to let a man take credit for all my hard work. So, I went to the newspaper instead."

"But why'd you do it, Darcy? Why'd you kill all those people? The victims, those men, were innocent."

"Innocent?" She laughed. "They were dirty. They wanted to make me dirty. I had to clean up the filth."

"Dirty, how? What did they do to you?"

"Smiled. Talked. Touched me. They wanted me to touch them, too. You never, never touch a man. You can never, never want his touch. If you do, the hand has to be made lifeless."

Obviously, this was the missing piece. Darcy had been attracted to her victims and for her, a sexual attraction was akin to a sin so black that death was the only remedy.

"What about Larry Walker? You lived with him in Las Vegas. You followed him to Pleasant Pines."

"Me? Follow him? Wyatt, I took you for a smarter man. I'd never follow the likes of Larry Walker anywhere. He followed me. He never wanted to come to Pleasant Pines. I don't blame him, either. It's too claustrophobic here. But I heard that you'd moved to Wyoming and I knew that you needed me, so I came."

"I don't need you, Darcy. I never have."

"That's the biggest lie I've ever heard."

"Why'd you kill Larry? Was he dirty, too?"

Darcy waved the question away. "Sometimes sacrifices have to be made. The Darkness told me to do it."

"What's the Darkness?" Wyatt asked. All he had to do was keep her talking until the RMJ team could get here.

And where in the hell are they? Goddammit, they should have been here by now!

Darcy smiled and flipped her hair over her shoulder. Was she flirting with Wyatt?

"You know the Darkness."

Maybe she was right. Maybe he did know the darkness. Gripping the rifle's stock tighter, Wyatt's finger caressed the trigger. A single shot and Darcy Owens would be no more. The case would be solved. Wyatt would have the truth and his vengeance with a single bullet.

The wind whipped around the schoolhouse, bringing with it a faint noise. A groan. A creaking. A cry.

"Everly!" Was she still alive? His gaze darted toward the doorway.

In that split instant, Darcy dipped low. The shotgun was in her grasp. Wyatt didn't think. By instinct alone he pulled the trigger. His aim wasn't as true as he hoped. The bullet struck Darcy in the shoulder. The power of the impact knocked her into the wall of the old schoolhouse, painting the worn wood red with her blood. The gun slipped from her grasp. She gripped the wound. Blood filled her hand and cascaded down her arm.

He aimed once more and fired. This time, the bullet tore through the hood of her car, destroying the engine.

Running past Darcy, he retrieved her gun. Coming to the threshold, Wyatt stopped short. The body of Carl Haak was sprawled on the floor, surrounded by a pool of blood, black as tar.

Just beyond hung Everly Baker. A rope was tight around her neck. Her eyelids fluttered. Was it a reflex in death or was Everly still alive?

After setting both weapons aside, Wyatt rushed forward. He grabbed Everly's torso and he took all her weight on his shoulder. He loosened the noose and felt the whisper of Everly's breath on his skin. In the distance, the sound of an approaching vehicle was unmistakable.

RMJ. *Finally.*

Withdrawing a knife from his pocket, he sawed through the rope that held Everly. Once she was free, he laid her on the floor. At the same moment, Marcus Jones, Julia McCloud, and Luis Martinez entered the old schoolhouse.

Sure, they were Marcus's crew, but Wyatt began to bark orders. "We need an ambulance," he said.

"Someone needs to provide first aid to Haak. And someone else has to take Darcy Owens into custody."

Four things happened at once. Julia kneeled next to the sheriff. Martinez removed a cell phone and placed a call. Marcus rushed from the room, apparently ready to apprehend Darcy. In the same instant, Wyatt searched for Everly's pulse. He felt a faint fluttering under his fingertips.

Thank God, she was alive.

Julia dropped back to her heels. The body of Sheriff Haak was unnaturally still. Looking at Wyatt, Julia shook her head. "He's gone," she said.

"We have an ambulance on the way," Martinez said. "How is she?" He meant Everly.

"Alive," said Wyatt. He studied Everly and watched her chest rise and fall. Tracing the angry, red welt around her throat he tried not to think of what would have happened if he'd been distracted by Darcy for a few minutes more.

The wail of a siren filled the quiet morning. "That's the ambulance," said Martinez. "I'll direct them in here."

Martinez passed Marcus at the door. Jones approached Wyatt. The other man's breathing was shallow and sweat coated his brow.

"What is it?" Julia asked.

"She's gone," said Marcus. "Darcy's escaped."

Wyatt was on his feet. "Escaped? That's impossible. She was wounded. I left her by the door."

"It's what I'm telling you, man. She's gone."

"And she wasn't by the door when we arrived," said Julia.

"Damn," Wyatt cursed. "We need to find her."

"We will," said Marcus.

His words were interrupted by two sets of paramedics who passed by with medical bags and stretchers. One group began to check for signs of life with the sheriff while the other tended to Everly.

"We will find Darcy…" said Marcus again.

"There is no *we*. She's *my* mess to clean up," said Wyatt. He moved to the door but couldn't help but look over his shoulder at Everly. She was alive now, but gravely wounded. What were the chances that she could survive a hanging?

"Finding the killer is *our* responsibility," said Marcus.

"Our?"

"Wyatt, you're on a team now. We are all taking a part in this investigation," said Marcus. "You stay here, and I'll take Julia and Martinez with me. If Darcy's as wounded as you say, then we should find her quickly."

Wyatt loathed the idea of leaving the capture to someone else. He wanted more than to see justice served—but also vengeance. All the same, maybe what Wyatt needed right now was a team.

Everly moaned and Wyatt turned to the sound.

"Go," he said to Marcus. "And good luck."

"Yeah," said Marcus, looking at Everly. Then he put a hand on Wyatt's shoulder. "You, too."

Without another word, the other man was gone.

The paramedics had placed Everly on a stretcher that was still flush to the ground. Two IVs were threaded into her hand.

"How is she?" Wyatt asked.

One of the paramedics answered. "We've gotten her stabilized—started both a saline drip and morphine for the pain. But we won't know anything conclusive until we can get her to the hospital and run some tests." The stretcher was lifted. Two sets of legs sprang out from the bottom and they began wheeling her toward the door.

Wyatt stayed at Everly's side as she was moved. He reached for her hand and wondered if she could feel his touch. He hoped like hell that she could. "I'm here," he said as they reached the rear doors to the ambulance. "And I'm not leaving."

Blind with pain, Darcy Owens stumbled through the woods. With each step her strength ebbed away, leaving her in a whirlpool of confusion and despair. Her foot caught, and she tripped, sprawling to the ground. She cried out in pain as her shoulder filled with fire.

Her lips were coated with dirt. She spat. Her spittle was brown with earth and red with blood.

"Get up," a voice snarled at her from behind.

Darcy used the last of her strength to flop to her back. The sun shone at him from behind, yet she recognized him even in shadow.

"Get up," he said again.

She began to quiver. Her father had been dead

for years. He couldn't be here, not now—not unless she was dead…and he had come to drag her to Hell.

"You aren't real," she said. Yes, that was it. She'd lost too much blood and was hallucinating. "You're a figment of my imagination."

He moved out of the shadows and kneeled next to Darcy. She clearly saw the golden flecks in the irises of his eyes. "Am I?" he asked. His stale breath washed over her cheek. It still smelled of whiskey and cigarette smoke.

She recalled other nights when she smelled the stench of the same breath. Darcy's stomach revolted, and she retched on the forest floor.

"Go away," she said. She swatted at him, using the last of her strength.

He grabbed her wrist, his fingers digging painfully into her flesh. "Does this feel like your imagination?"

She jerked her hand away. "What do you want?"

"Now you listen to me, girlie. You need to get up and move."

"I can't," she said. "I'm just so tired."

"If you stay here, they're going to catch you."

"I don't care," she said. Her eyelids were heavy, so heavy. Too heavy.

And then her father disappeared with the mist.

Darcy floated, as if above her body. The woods melted away and for a moment, she was in Las Vegas. As a child, Darcy sought shelter in the Darkness. As an adult, she thought it was no longer needed and hoped the desert sun would chase it all away. What she hadn't understood was that night in the desert was black as pitch. It was then that the Darkness would envelop her. The first time had been an accident. She hadn't meant to hurt him—much less let the Darkness take control.

She'd been lying out by the pool, the noonday sun warming her and filling her with light. Darcy had almost felt normal, whole and human.

A shadow passed over her face.

"Hey," a deep voice had said.

She shielded her eyes and looked up. He stood there, looking down at her, and gave a slow smile.

Her stomach summersaulted, and despite the desert heat, gooseflesh covered her arms.

"Hey," she said.

"You look lonely," he said. "Mind if I join you?"

Darcy felt a smile pull up one corner of her mouth. She ran a hand over her mouth, smothering the ridiculous expression.

"It's a free country."

"Ouch." The man placed his hand on his heart, as if mortally wounded.

This time, Darcy laughed.

"I'll take that as a *yes*," he said, sprawling out on a chaise beside her.

"So, you live here? In Vegas?" he asked.

She nodded, unable to think of something to say.

"It must be great," he said.

Darcy shrugged.

"Listen, I don't want to be a creep. If you want me

to leave—just say so. It's just that you're so pretty, I couldn't help myself."

Darcy stared forward. She'd heard the words before and felt sick with the familiarity. "You're so pretty," her father had said. "I can't help myself."

After, Darcy's mother told her that what happened was all Darcy's fault. She was dirty, and wholly to blame.

It was then that Darkness had come to protect her and keep her safe.

That day, by the pool, the sun had glinted off the water. It was so bright that tears streamed from her eyes, even now.

"Maybe we should hang out this evening," Darcy had said, in a voice that wasn't hers. It had been the Darkness that had invited the man to stay.

The Darkness waited for the nighttime sky to unfold—a chasm of nothing. He drank too much, touched her, kissed her. She couldn't let herself be violated—not again. That's when the Darkness took over. It told her to ply him with more drinks, even after he asked for water. It told her to tear a two-dollar bill in half and put part of the bill in his wallet, using the same money her father used when paying for her silence. The Darkness told her to take the man to the desert, leave him and never look back.

Darcy's shoulder throbbed. She longed to close her eyes and never open them again. There was a rustle in the brush. Using the last of her strength, she turned her head. It was a hulking figure, covered in thick black fur. It growled, the rumbling sound low and menacing.

It took a step toward her and then another. Its eyes were dark brown, almost black, and in them…she saw her own distorted reflection. She was beaten, bruised and certainly no match for the beast. Darcy turned away, no longer caring what happened.

Julia McCloud had spent years in the Army. She was one of the few women accepted to Ranger School. She'd served in combat, hunting the Taliban in the Hindukush mountain range. Most recently, she'd assisted in the apprehension of a Russian Drug Lord in Denver. Yet, after four hours of hunting through the woods, Julia had to wonder how hard was it to find a lone and injured woman?

More than that, she had to admit that she'd lost the trail as soon as they started. "This is a total goat-rope," she said, using the euphemism for what she really wanted to say. "She's gone. Yet, there's no such thing as magic. People don't disappear."

"Is that it?" asked Martinez. "Are we giving up and going back?"

"Rangers don't quit," she said.

Martinez removed a water bottle from his backpack. After taking a drink, he shrugged. Julia read the gesture as *have it your way*.

"By now," said Marcus, "other teams have to be looking for Darcy Owens."

In their haste to find the killer, the RMJ operatives had set out before any other law enforcement officials had arrived. It meant that RMJ led the chase, but it also put them at a disadvantage. They lacked communication and coordination with the other teams. For all they knew, Darcy Owens had been found already.

"One more mile," she said, while scanning the surroundings. There, less than a quarter of a click to the east, was a flash of red. "What's that?" Julia asked before doubling-timing it toward what she had seen.

Martinez and Marcus were on her heels.

Snarled in a tree branch was a small scrap of fabric. At one time, it had been white, but was now covered in blood.

"You think that belongs to Darcy?" Marcus asked.

"The fabric is still tacky, so the blood is fresh," said Martinez. "It hasn't been here long. Maybe a few hours, so I'd say it was a possibility."

Julia examined a nearby snapped twig. The break was still wet with sap. She concurred with Martinez's assessment. "Two hours at the most."

"That means she's close," said Marcus.

Once again, Julia scanned the woods. There were no other broken branches. No underbrush was disturbed. There weren't even drops of blood on the ground. Sure, Darcy was close, but where? There were a million different directions she could have gone.

Even though she'd been honest in saying that Rangers never quit, she also knew something else to be true. It took an Army to win a war.

"Can you get in touch with the state police?" Julia

asked Martinez. She already knew the answer. He was the one carrying the satellite phone.

"Sure can," he said.

"Maybe it's time we bring in some air power," suggested Julia. "With heat sensing radar, they should be able to see everything we can't."

"In finding a trail to follow," said Marcus, "we've done good work. But we aren't done with this case. Until Darcy Owens is found, dead or alive, RMJ will be on the hunt."

Chapter 16

For almost twenty-two hours, Wyatt sat in the hospital, next to Everly's bedside. He drank stale coffee, ate take-out food from Sally's and waited for two things.

First was for Everly to wake up. The second was for news that the team had captured Darcy Owens. It seemed as though the killer, wounded though she was, had walked away from the old schoolhouse and simply vanished.

Of course, there were rumors and theories, supplied by the operatives from RMJ. They ran from the absurd—she'd been hauled off by the same wolves Axl Baker had been sent to photograph—to the probable—she died of her wounds and the harsh Wyoming wilderness had claimed her body.

Then there was the single theory that Wyatt thought was most likely.

Darcy Owens had help during her escape.

That brought up a new question—who would help her? Finding the answer was the next mystery to be solved.

Marcus had also briefed Wyatt on Darcy's background. As it turns out, the Pleasant Pines district attorney, Chloe Ryder, had been a college intern in Darcy's high school. The DA had provided a treasure trove of information about the killer as an adolescent.

More than providing updates, RMJ had proved to be stalwart teammates, bringing Wyatt all those takeout meals. In fact, Marcus had even offered to stay at Wyatt's place and take care of Gus.

The news about Everly was equally vague and unsatisfying. Since Everly's heart beat on its own, and she didn't need any respiratory intervention, Doc Lambert felt that she'd eventually wake.

When?

That was a question he couldn't answer.

Despite the fact that Wyatt wanted Everly taken to a larger hospital in Cheyenne, she didn't have a next-of-kin to contact regarding her care.

It left her medical insurance reviewing treatment options for Everly. The first day came and went and they hadn't contacted Doc Lambert with a plan.

For hours on end, Wyatt watched. Each time Everly drew breath, he held his own, fearful that it might be her last. But Everly stayed alive and it left Wyatt with nothing to do, beyond wait and hope.

At the end of the first day, Everly stirred in her sleep. Wyatt rushed to her side on legs that were fatigued and cramped from the rigid little hospital chairs.

Clasping her hand, he said, "Everly. It's Wyatt. Can you hear me?"

She turned to him and blinked, before closing her eyes and letting out a deep breath. As quickly as he had moved to her side, he was on his feet again and at the door to her hospital room.

"Nurse," he called, both hopeful and alarmed. "Get the doctor. Everly opened her eyes."

The nurse didn't have to do anything. Doc Lambert must've heard Wyatt and the older man came running from a side corridor.

Everly was given a complete physical and within an hour, she was proclaimed to be on the mend—physically, at least. "I don't want you traveling for more than a week," said Doc Lambert. "And for the next few days I need you to stay in the hospital for observation."

"Thanks, Doc," said Wyatt. He had no doubt that he would care for Everly until she recovered.

"Call the nurse if you need anything," he said.

"Will do."

Once the doctor left, Everly swallowed. The red welt around her neck had turned to a purple bruise that was slowly fading to yellow and green. "Darcy Owens?" she asked, her voice a hoarse whisper.

Wyatt shook his head. "She got away. But she won't get far. Everyone in the state is looking for her. Hell, she's the lead story on every newscast. She can't stay hidden long."

Biting her bottom lip, Everly nodded. "Sheriff Haak?"

"Sorry," he said, his voice thick with regret. "He didn't make it."

"How is it that I'm alive, then?" Each time she spoke, her voice became stronger and louder. "I remember the moment that Darcy kicked away the stool. Everything went black and I knew I was dead." Swallowing, she asked, "Who saved me? You?"

Wyatt shrugged. "I wish I would've gotten there earlier…" There was so much more that Wyatt wanted to say, but even now, he couldn't find the words.

"How long have I been in the hospital?" she asked.

"Almost a whole day."

Everly's eyes went wide. "You have to tell me everything."

Wyatt began to speak, ready to use the old cliché—*there's not much to tell*. But that would've been a lie.

Because of the information brought to him by Marcus Jones, Wyatt finally felt as if he understood everything that had motivated Darcy Owens' murderous acts.

"Do you remember Chloe Ryder?"

"The DA we met at Sally's?" asked Everly. "Sure."

He then spent the next several minutes outlining the story he had been given. As a college student studying social work, Chloe had been an intern at Darcy's school. A conversation between the young women had left Chloe uneasy and she suspected abuse at home. As per legal requirements, she reported her suspicions to her supervisor. They questioned Darcy, who denied everything and said that Chloe had been mistaken. Since there was no evidence, no action was taken.

A few weeks later, Darcy's father was found dead.

"Let me guess," said Everly. "He drank too much and got lost outside."

"Your guess would be right. But there's more. A few weeks following, her mother committed suicide. Death by hanging. Everyone assumed that her mother was broken-hearted over losing her husband. After that, Darcy dropped out of school and wasn't heard from again."

Everly shuddered. "Is she recreating the accidental deaths of both her parents?"

"Could be," said Wyatt. "Or perhaps, those two were Darcy's original victims and she's just been repeating the same crimes again and again."

"I don't know what to say." Everly's voice was weak again.

"Just rest," he said. "I'll be here when you wake up."

Everly smiled. "Thanks."

Her eyes drifted closed. After a moment, she opened them again. "What do we do now?"

"We focus on you," Wyatt said. He reached for her palm. "You are going to rest and get better."

She stroked the back of his hand. "And after that? What then?"

That was the exact question Wyatt had been asking himself for almost an entire day. "It's not safe for you to travel yet, with Darcy still at large. As far as we know, you're the only person she's tried to kill who survived. Until she's caught, I'm not leaving your side. Once you can travel, I'll go back to Chicago. And after she's captured..." Pausing, he looked at his hands. Was he really ready to commit to Everly? He knew damn well that he wasn't going to be able to let her walk out of his life again. He spoke. "After she's captured, I'll stay, that is, if you'll have me."

"What about the search for Darcy? Don't you want to get back out there and find her?"

"Sure," said Wyatt. "But sometimes priorities change."

Everly shook her head. "I don't believe for a minute that you want to be in Chicago with me while the search for Darcy is happening in Wyoming."

"What I want doesn't matter anymore," he said. "I need to keep you safe. Dammit, Everly. You've become everything to me. I thought I lost you once." His mind was filled with an image of her seemingly lifeless body as it hung from the rafters. Closing his eyes, he waited for the picture and ensuing feeling of loss and loneliness to pass. "I never want to lose you again."

Everly reached for his arm. "I'm not going anywhere," she said. "You and I, we're a team—a family. It doesn't matter whether we're in Chicago or here. There's a lot to love about Pleasant Pines—like you."

Wyatt's chest expanded until it ached. He took a knee beside her bed. Brushing the hair from her forehead, Wyatt placed a kiss on her brow. "I love you so much that it hurts."

"Oh, Wyatt," she said, tracing his jaw with a light touch. "I love you, too."

"So that's it?" he asked. "You'll stay?"

"There's no place else I'd rather be than here, with you." She paused and smiled. "Well, maybe not in the hospital, but you get my point."

He did indeed.

He drew her into an embrace and his mouth laid claim to hers. And there, in the small and stuffy hospital room, their life could start fresh.

The hunt could wait.

Epilogue

Two weeks later

Wyatt sat behind the desk and looked to the window. There was nothing beyond opaque glass for him to see. He missed the view from his house of the Rocky Mountains and the clear blue sky. At the same time, he reveled in his newfound purpose.

Before Everly was released from the hospital, Marcus had again asked Wyatt to join RMJ. Without hesitation, he accepted.

Chloe Ryder had hired RMJ to serve as the investigative body for the district attorney's office and Wyatt's first job would be to lead the hunt for the still at-large killer.

"Knock, knock."

He recognized the voice without having to look.

"Everly." Wyatt sat at his desk, set within a cubicle in a large and open work space. Aside from Wyatt, the room was empty. All other operatives were out.

"I know that you are still getting settled at work, but I wanted to bring a little something for your office." She held out a white box with a big red bow. "I told Marcus I would be stopping by and he let me in," she continued, explaining how she had circumvented RMJ's extreme security.

"Thanks," he said as he lifted the lid. Inside was a framed photo of Everly and Gus, with the Rocky Mountains serving as the backdrop. His family. His home. Wyatt's throat tightened a little.

"Just a little reminder of what's waiting for you at the end of the workday," she said. "And speaking of workdays, I have my first Pleasant Pines client."

In the weeks since she decided to stay, she'd joined a public relations firm in Laramie, forty-five minutes south of town. It was a hefty commute and she planned to work from home as much as possible. Still, he was impressed that she'd already landed a local client.

"Already? Who?"

"The sheriff's department," she said. "The media coverage they've been getting has been awful. I have a meeting in a little bit with Chloe Ryder. Once we present our side of the events, the story will become more balanced."

Everly paused and Wyatt knew what she was thinking. He answered the question before she had a chance to ask. "There's nothing new in the search for Darcy or her body," he said.

Everly gave a quick nod. "I wish we knew something," she said. "That's all."

He did as well, yet he said nothing. He set the photo on his desk. "I like the space better already."

"See you tonight?" she said.

He wrapped his arms around Everly's waist and pulled her onto his lap. Pressing his lips to hers, he gave her a languid kiss. "See you tonight."

He wanted to hold her forever, not just because she felt so damned nice in his arms, but because Darcy Owens was still out there—somewhere. Until they found the killer and put her in prison, nobody would be safe.

The hunt had begun again.

This time it was more than about public safety and justice. For Wyatt, catching Darcy Owens was a personal fight. And he didn't intend to lose.

Darcy awoke with a start. Her throat was parched. Her eyes were swollen. Her shoulder throbbed, and the stench of rot surrounded her. She sat up. Blinding pain split her skull and she leaned back with a groan.

"You up?" a deep male voice asked.

She opened her eyes the slightest bit. A hulking figure stood at the end of her bed. His face was covered in wiry, black hair. His eyes were just tiny dots and his mouth nothing more than a slash.

"You up?" he asked again.

"Yes," she croaked.

"Drink this," he said. A large and powerful arm snaked behind Darcy's back and lifted her. A cup was pressed to her lips and water trickled down her throat.

The man stepped away and she sank into the pillow.

"What happened?" she asked, her mind foggy.

"You were shot," said the man. "I found you in the woods and brought you here."

It all became clear and Darcy's pulse began to race. Her shoulder pounded with each beat of her heart. "Where am I? How long have I been here?"

"You're in my bunker," the man said. "I saw the news. It looks like you're in a heap of trouble, so I haven't said nothing to the police."

Darcy's pulse slowed, more confused than thankful. "Why are you hiding me?"

The hulking man said, "I've been in trouble with the law before. I won't ever help those bastards."

Her eyes began to drift closed. She was still so tired.

Wake up, the Darkness whispered in Darcy's ear. She pried her lids open and her hand went to her throat. Cold and hard, a chain was bolted to her neck. Icy terror dropped into her middle.

The large man grinned as her eyes went wide.

"Who are you?" she asked. "What have you done?"

"As far as who I am," said the man. "I'm Billy Dawson. And what have I done?" He scratched his wiry beard. "Since I saved you, you owe me."

Darcy's breath was trapped in her chest. She wasn't sure she'd ever be able to breathe again.

Look, the Darkness whispered in Darcy's ear. There, in the corner, was an ax. The blade glinted in the firelight.

If she wanted to survive, she'd have to do more than embrace the Darkness, but allow it to take over completely.

"You're right," she said to the man. "You did rescue me. Without you, I'd either be dead or in jail."

He smiled, thinking that he'd somehow won.

Flicking her gaze quickly to the ax, Darcy smiled, as well. Just as Billy had been her savior, she was certain to be his damnation.

* * * * *

The operatives of Rocky Mountain Justice are on the hunt for Darcy Owens! Look for the next thrilling installment of Wyoming Nights, Jennifer D. Bokal's miniseries for Harlequin Romantic Suspense.

Coming soon, wherever Harlequin books and ebooks are sold.

Get 4 FREE REWARDS!

We'll send you 2 FREE Books plus 2 FREE Mystery Gifts.

Harlequin® Romantic Suspense books feature heart-racing sensuality and the promise of a sweeping romance set against the backdrop of suspense.

FREE Value Over **$20**

YES! Please send me 2 FREE Harlequin® Romantic Suspense novels and my 2 FREE gifts (gifts are worth about $10 retail). After receiving them, if I don't wish to receive any more books, I can return the shipping statement marked "cancel." If I don't cancel, I will receive 4 brand-new novels every month and be billed just $4.99 per book in the U.S. or $5.74 per book in Canada. That's a savings of at least 12% off the cover price! It's quite a bargain! Shipping and handling is just 50¢ per book in the U.S. and $1.25 per book in Canada.* I understand that accepting the 2 free books and gifts places me under no obligation to buy anything. I can always return a shipment and cancel at any time. The free books and gifts are mine to keep no matter what I decide.

240/340 HDN GNMZ

Name (please print)

Address   Apt. #

City   State/Province   Zip/Postal Code

Mail to the **Reader Service:**
IN U.S.A.: P.O. Box 1341, Buffalo, NY 14240-8531
IN CANADA: P.O. Box 603, Fort Erie, Ontario L2A 5X3

Want to try 2 free books from another series? Call 1-800-873-8635 or visit www.ReaderService.com.

HRS20

SPECIAL EXCERPT FROM

⬧ HARLEQUIN®

ROMANTIC suspense

*State Trooper Kelly Roberts joins Special Agent
Tony Lazzaro's task force, determined to bring down
a cybercriminal preying on young victims. Solving
this case is a chance for redemption. If Kelly catches
the killer, she'll be one step closer to solving her best
friend's abduction. She never expects to fall for Tony...*

*Read on for a sneak preview of
Dana Nussio's next book in the True Blue miniseries,
Her Dark Web Defender.*

"Ready to try this again?"

"Absolutely."

Kelly met his gaze with a confidence he didn't expect. Was she trying to prove something to him? Trying to convince him he'd made a mistake by shielding her before?

"Okay, let's chat."

The conversation appeared to have slowed during the time he'd gone for coffee, but the moment Tony typed his first line, his admirers were back. Didn't any of these guys have a day job?

It didn't take long before one of them sent a private message at the bottom of the screen. GOOD TIME GUY wasn't all that shy about escalating the conversation quickly, either. Kelly took over the keyboard, and when the guy suggested a voice chat, she didn't even look Tony's way before she accepted.

"Hey, your voice is rougher than I expected," she said into the microphone.

Only then did she glance sidelong at Tony. He nodded his approval. He'd been right to give her a second chance. Dawson and the others didn't need to know about the other day, the part at the office or anything that happened later. Kelly would be great at this.

When the conversation with GOOD TIME GUY didn't seem to be going anywhere, they ended that interaction and accepted another offer for a personal chat. She navigated that one with BOY AT HEART and even a repeat one with BIG DADDY with the skill of someone who'd been on the task force a year rather than days.

Her breathing might have been a little halting, and she might have tightened her grip on the microphone, but she was powering through, determined to tease details from each of the possible suspects that they might be able to use to track them.

Tony found he had to admit something else. He'd been wrong about Kelly Roberts. She was stronger than he'd expected her to be. Maybe even fearless. And he was dying to know what had made her that way.

Don't miss
Her Dark Web Defender *by Dana Nussio,*
available November 2019 wherever
Harlequin® Romantic Suspense
books and ebooks are sold.

Harlequin.com

Need an adrenaline rush from nail-biting tales
(and irresistible males)?

Check out **Harlequin Intrigue®**,
Harlequin® Romantic Suspense and
Love Inspired® Suspense books!

New books available every month!

CONNECT WITH US AT:

Facebook.com/groups/HarlequinConnection

 Facebook.com/HarlequinBooks

 Twitter.com/HarlequinBooks

 Instagram.com/HarlequinBooks

Pinterest.com/HarlequinBooks

ReaderService.com

 **HARLEQUIN®**

**ROMANCE WHEN
YOU NEED IT**

SGENRE20

Love Harlequin romance?

DISCOVER.

Be the first to find out about promotions, news and exclusive content!

 Facebook.com/HarlequinBooks

Twitter.com/HarlequinBooks

 Instagram.com/HarlequinBooks

Pinterest.com/HarlequinBooks

ReaderService.com

EXPLORE.

Sign up for the Harlequin e-newsletter and download a free book from any series at **TryHarlequin.com.**

CONNECT.

Join our Harlequin community to share your thoughts and connect with other romance readers!

acebook.com/groups/HarlequinConnection

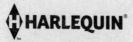

**ROMANCE WHEN
YOU NEED IT**

HSOCIAL2018